Shattered Ice

Sasha R.C.

Shattered Ice

Formatting/Editor: MJ Bryant

Author Assistant/Development: Kaylea Fink

Cover by: The Author Buddy

Contents

21. Brad

22. Cole

23. Natalie

24. Alexa

25. Brad

26. Cole

27. Natalie

28. Alexa

29. Brad

30. Cole

31. Natalie

32. Alexa

33. Brad

34. Cole

35. Alexa

36. Cole

37. Natalie

38. Brad

39. Alexa

40. Brad

41. Alexa

42. Brad

43. Cole

44. Alexa

Author Note

Hello, My Fellow Readers,

This is a Dark Hockey Romance.

This book dives right in from the start and contains some themes and topics that may be hard for some to handle. There may be things within this book that might trigger and be uncomfortable for some readers. Please make sure that you read ALL the warnings listed on the following pages—your mental health matters.

If you are looking for a slow burn, build-up to obsession, and love that makes sense, this book is not for you.

Please remember that this book is a work of fiction and is not based on actual events. Please read the Trigger/Content Warnings.

THIS IS NOT A SLOW BURN! THIS IS NOT A BUILD-UP TO OBSESSION! THE LOVE INSIDE THIS BOOK DOES NOT MAKE SENSE, AND GUESS WHAT? IT IS NOT MEANT TO!

IF YOU ARE LOOKING FOR A LOGICAL DARK ROMANCE>>>THIS IS NOT IT!!

Trigger/Content Warnings

This is a Dark Hockey Romance.

This book has dark elements and themes, including sexual, physical, psychological, and mental abuse, gaslighting, foul language, grooming and conditioning of MFC.

Other dark themes and elements include Sexual Assault and Suicide.

Drug and alcohol use.

This book is fiction. There are no real events or people depicted in this book. This book is all fantasy.

I want to make it clear. I do not condone anything that happens in this book.

Please use caution. You know yourself best.

This book is intended for mature adults over the age of 18.

I do not write perfect characters. I write them as I see them in my head, including how they think, behave, and what they say internally.

This book is based on the sexual connection and desire between the characters and is not focused on the world around them or senseless dialogue.

If you are looking for a slow burn, build-up to obsession, and love that makes sense, this book is not for you.

THIS IS NOT A SLOW BURN! THIS IS NOT A BUILD-UP TO OBSESSION! THE LOVE INSIDE THIS BOOK DOES NOT MAKE SENSE, AND GUESS WHAT? IT IS NOT MEANT TO! IF YOU ARE LOOKING FOR A LOGICAL DARK ROMANCE>>>THIS IS NOT IT!!

This is your second warning.

Special Dedication

Kay-Author Assistant/Development/Alpha Reader: Where to begin. You have been such an amazing, strong foundation for me. Thank you for being my North Star and walking side by side with me through this crazy madness called life. I appreciate you for all the hard work you put into being my AA and taking the time to read my books. Thank you so much for all of your suggestions. I want you to know that you are appreciated. Thank you for being you.

Mel-Formatting/Editor: Thank you so much for everything that you do. Thank you for going through this crazy process with me. I appreciate you for all the long hours, hard work, and phone calls and for falling in love with my stories as much as I have.

My ARC/Street Team: You are all so amazing. Thank you for signing up, promoting, reviewing, and always being willing to read my crazy stories.To all my readers: Thank you so much for

taking a chance and reading my books and diving into my crazy, dark, smutty romance world. I appreciate all of you and could not have made my dream a reality without you.

The Author Buddy: Thank you for the 3-D graphics, all of the new covers, and for going on this crazy ride with me.

Acknowledgments

Karen Prosser: For being my best friend, my soundboard. Thank you for always being willing to listen to all of my new ideas for my books, giving me new ideas for more books, and helping me with the character names. I couldn't have done this without you. Thank you for being you.

Sunflower Downer: For always being there for me, making me laugh, and encouraging me to follow my dreams. Thank you for believing in me and always being there when I need you.

Jamie Williams: For being so inspirational. You are so amazing. Thank you for all of your support. Thank you for believing in me. Thank you for being my friend.

Playlist

"Narcissist" by Lauren Spencer Smith

"Locksmith" by Sadie Jean

While You're At It" by Jessie Murph

"Where You Belong" by Matt Hansen

"Paralyzed" by NF

"Declined" by Britton

"Little Bit Better" by Caleb Hearn, ROSIE

"You Were Mine" by Forest Black

"Seeing You With Other Girls" by Natalie Jane

"You'll Be Alright, Kid" by Alex Warren

"Knees" by Bebe Rexha

"Bigger Person" by Lauren Spencer Smith

"Who Do I Call Now(Hellbent)" by Sofia Camara

"it is what it is" by Abe Parker

"Versions of Forever " by Matt Hansen

"Can You Hear Me" by Munn

"Start Over" by Jessica Baio, Mykyl

"Leave Me Alone" by Logan Michael

"Hate You" by Jordi

"I hope ur miserable until ur dead" by Nessa Barrett

"Can You Hold Me" by NF, Britt Nicole

"Can't Miss You Anymore" by Avery Anna

"Back to Friends" by Lauren Spencer Smith

"She's an Actor" by Austin Giorgio

"Where Do We Go From Here?" by Caleb Hearn

"strangers again" by Matt Hansen

"Empty Eyes" by Munn

"someday" by Jessica Baio

"Love is Gone – Acoustic" by SLANDER, Dylan Matthew

"One More I Love You" by Alex Warren

"Last Man Standing" by Livingston

"If You Died Today" by Natalie Jane

"Narcissist" by Avery Anna

"Fingers Crossed" by Lauren Spencer Smith

"A Drop in the Ocean" by Ron Pope

"Would Anyone Care" by Citizen Soldier

"you broke me first" by Tate McRae

"the reason i hate home" by Munn

"Sad Song" by We The Kings feat Elena Coats

"Antidote" by Faith Marie

"Silent Scream" by Anna Blue

"Care About Me" by JESSIA

"Loved Me That Way" by Lauren Duski

"Starlight" by Sofia Camara

"Flowers" by Lauren Spencer Smith

"What Hurts The Most" by Rascal Flatts

"If I Surrender" by Citizen Soldier

"I Lost Myself In Loving You" by Jamie Miller

"Loved Us More" by Munn

"Wasting All These Tears" by Cassadee Pope

https://open.spotify.com/playlist/1BjFEDndDlxOPFg
mR5uN8e?si=MBfjpEPHSjShjfVVbyEzRQ

Please Read

Hello, My Smutty Dark Romance Lovers,

This is for those who love sexy, tattooed, possessive, no-boundaries kind of men.

This is for those of you who need a new kind of Beauty and the Beast Retelling. The story told within these pages is very Dark. I use the words Fuck and Fucking A LOT. They are, in fact, two of my favorite words. I want to inform you that the words Fuck, Fucking, and any other lovely cuss words I use are not used for dramatic effect. This is the way me and my characters talk.

Have fun getting lost in this smutty fucking goodness :)

I do not write perfect characters.

This book is based on the sexual connection and desire between the characters and is NOT focused on the world around them or senseless dialogue.

If you are looking for a slow burn, build-up to obsession, and love that makes sense, this book is not for you.

THIS IS NOT A SLOW BURN!THIS IS NOT A BUILD-UP TO OBSESSION!THE LOVE INSIDE THIS BOOK DOES NOT MAKE SENSE, AND GUESS WHAT? IT IS NOT MEANT TO!IF YOU ARE LOOKING FOR A LOGICAL DARK ROMANCE>>>THIS IS NOT IT!!

You now have been Warned three times!!!

Prologue

Alexa - 4 Years Ago

Everything has a beginning, the starting point of where they lose who they were and become someone else entirely. This is the point for me where my fantasies of being passed around have put me in a situation where the word "no" means absolutely nothing and they just take what they want.

"Don't cry sweetheart, we know you want our cocks," he says with a chuckle as he continues to hold my throat from behind, his lips against my ear.

I can smell the booze and weed on him; it makes me want to gag. Tears are escaping my eyes and rolling down my face, making me feel even more defeated. The vodka shots I downed not too long ago are making my stomach roll, and his words are echoing inside my head.

Fucking is easy, especially when there are no strings attached. But these men make me want to run, run far away.

"Please, I think I am going to get sick," I whimper as he tightens his hold on my throat.

I hear movement in front of me and I open my eyes to find his two friends standing in front of me with nothing but lust and malice in their eyes. Before I can utter a sound, they both reach out and roughly grab my breasts, squeezing and fondling me through my black crop top.

There is no way I am going to get out of this, but i have to try.

"I don't want this," I plead, making them all chuckle darkly.

The man behind me, presses his lips are to my ear as he presses his free hand against my stomach, pulling me back into him. I can feel his already hard cock against my ass.

"Your words say no, but your body, sweetheart, says yes," he whispers.

I tense as his hand slides down my body and underneath my leggings. I try to move, but he tightens his hold on me. My heart is racing as I slam my eyes shut.

No amount of booze can help me escape this; I am trapped by my own making.

"Be our good little whore and get on your knees," he whispers.

Squeezing my eyes shut, more tears escape down my cheeks. I refuse to let them see the pain they are causing me.

A scream leaves me as I am yanked towards the couch. The man holding me keeps his grip on me. I can hear him yank his belt off, and the metal-on-metal zipping sounds echo loudly around me. He pulls me onto his bare lap with a deep groan.

I don't know how this got so out of hand, but between the booze, weed, and the racing of my heart, I can't get control of myself.

He roughly pushes his cock into my pussy, the burn making me scream out, but it doesn't stop him. If anything, it spurs him on. I can feel his friends' hands all over my body as the man I am sitting on starts thrusting up into me. This is a weird position, but he doesn't seem to care.

He is getting what he wants.

A piece of my soul.

Even though my mind is fucking screaming at my body to stop, their touches make my skin feel light up, and my pussy pulse with need.

My fucking body is betraying me, egging them on.

I guess they are right; I am a little whore.

They are ripping me apart from the inside, and they don't care.

No one cares.

Not even me, as my soul shatters like ice.

Chapter 1
Alexa

I am so late, so freaking late.

I shake my head as I pull into the hospital parking lot, pulling into the first parking spot I see. Turning off my car I grab my three bags and slide out trying to keep a tight grip on my coffee, but I guess it wasn't tight enough, because as I turn to shut the door with my side, my coffee hits the corner of the car door and spills down the front of me.

"Son of a turkey, bird shit," I curse under my breath as I use my hip to finish shutting the door. I turn and see Elly standing a few feet away, her eyes are wide, as I huff towards her and the back entrance to the ER.

A chuckle leaves her as I stop at her side and take a deep breath.

I turn and look at her. She is a little shorter than me, with her wavy grey hair up in a messy bun. She is the mother of the ER. She is kind and funny and is always there to help when you need it.

Like right now, she gives me a nod and slowly hands me her coffee, taking the empty coffee cup from my hand.

"I think you need this more than me, Alex," she says with empathy in her eyes.

This woman is so dang sweet. Being around her makes my teeth hurt.

She gently bumps her shoulder against my arm, gesturing for me to head into the ER. This is not the career I thought I would do; in fact, it is nothing close to what I want to be doing, but I didn't want to be anywhere near my parents. Unluckily for me, what I really want to do, they are right smack in the middle of the industry.

Taking a deep breath, I quickly make my way to the doors, swiping my badge against the lock. It turns green, and the sliding doors open quickly. As soon as they do, the smell of blood, tears, and sweat enters my nose.

I hate and love the smell of this place; it is my escape from my world. This place allows me to be in control. I know my job, and I do it well.

This job is very demanding of all of us. It involves long hours, little time for friends or social lift, and there are limited amounts of time for food or sleep. We are all addicted to the rush that it brings.

I had to find a new type of escape after I got sober — well, not completely sober, but sober enough to finish school and get this job. I don't have time to fuck, smoke, and drink anymore, but I have done that on purpose.

I make my way into the employee locker room and stop in front of my locker. I quickly enter the code and open the locker, taking a breath as I put my bags inside. I slam the locker shut, grab my folders, and make my way back out to the noisy, overcrowded ER.

Charleston, South Carolina. This town is old, beautiful, and breathtaking, but with beauty also comes pain and chaos. The NHL is the most dominant sport in our state and in this town. North Carolina is the home base for the professionals in the league. If you don't know what the NHL is, it stands for the National Hockey League. There are other sports here as well, but the most dominant is the ice.

Where there are athletes like that, there are injuries, fights, and blood, which is why I chose this ER. I had to get away from the rush of New York City, and this place just looked so peaceful. Plus, I have never fucked or been passed around by anyone in this state, so it was a clean slate for me, a do over, a new beginning. I moved here three months ago, and have been able to stay out of trouble.

I walk up to the desk and grab the first set of folders. There are patients waiting, crying, and screaming. Tonight is going to be a fun night, to say the least.

Here we go!

It's only seven hours into my shift, and I have already had to stop four fights and had four patients with gun-shot wounds, who thankfully all survived. There has been a shift in the type of patients over the past hour and the majority of them are athletes and their friends with various complaints from broken bones to what could possibly be STDs.

I grab my shaker cup and begin shaking the contents, and turn around, leaning my hip against the counter to watch the other nurses and doctors try to sort out the rush of men coming into the ER. I twist the cap and take a big drink.

Holy cow!

I force the liquid down my throat, feeling my stomach turn. I must make a face because several people giggle as I look down at the drink.

"Stupid protein drink," I snap, shaking my head.

Lumps, freaking lumps.

I swear I shook it up. In fact, I remember just moments ago shaking up the drink. I am still trying to swallow and not gag at the same time.

I love gagging, don't get me wrong, but not like this, not for this reason. But I have to force myself to ingest this. If I don't, I will be the one who will need a feeding tube and an IV drip.

I take the rest of the drink down and put my bottle down, grabbing another set of patient folders, making my way quickly over to room #14.

I look over the report: another bar fight; I swear. Most of the people we get in the ER have to do with drinking, fighting, and bars. I don't judge, not with the past I come from, but man, they have to have a limit, right? Some of these guys I have seen every weekend for the past three months that I have been here.

I shake my head and take a deep breath as I walk into the room and close the door. Seven hours down and seven more to go. Most nurses do 14-hour shifts. We are all addicted to the rush; I am just addicted to the distraction it brings.

I stop for a moment, looking at the first name, and look up from the folder. My heart stops as my eyes settle on the man sitting at the table waiting for me.

Dear Jesus.

I have never seen a man so gorgeous in my life, and I have been with a lot of men. This man has blond hair that is longer on the top and shaved on the sides. I can tell he has used mousse to keep it back.

Damn.

He is looking down at his phone, his fingers moving quickly as I take him in. He is wearing a pair of black slacks and black dress-up shoes. His suit jacket is lying across his lap, and the black button-up shirt is tight against his body. I can tell he has a nice body—not like the NHL players, more like a swimmer's body.

He is beyond attractive, and by the looks of his watch and the diamond ring on his right index finger, he has money.. Most people in this community are wealthy; I am finding out.

My heart races as I take him in, needing to see his eyes.

I am in so much trouble.

Chapter 2
Brad

Ilook up from my phone at the nurse that is standing a few feet away from me. I slowly lower my phone as I see her mouth is slightly open, and she is holding what I am assuming is my file tightly around her chest.

Her dark purpose scrubs make this dull ass room a little brighter. She has thick, big black glasses on, making her piercing forest green eyes more dominant and bright. I can feel my cock twitch in my jeans.

Fucking hell.

She is a smaller build, roughly 5 '3, and maybe 115 pounds soaking wet. Her scrubs are a tight fit, showing me that her body is fit enough to make her have curves in all the right places, but not enough to make my jaw drop.

I take in her face. Her skin is fucking perfect. The only evidence of makeup is the black eyeliner. Her dark brown hair is up in a messy bun; pieces of her hair shape her face.

She slowly lowers the folder, enough for me to see she has decent-sized breasts. I like bigger breasts, but her size fits her overall and the natural, I don't give a fuck look she has going on is intriguing.

I take in a deep breath. Her perfume fills my nose with what smells a bit like the ocean and something that is unique to her. She could be gorgeous if she put in the time to do so, she in fact, could be breathtaking.

This woman just needs a little guidance. Every woman needs a man to lead them and tell them what to do. After all, women don't do well on their own. They need a man like me to take control.

I am good at taking control, I can't stand not being obeyed. Disrespect isn't something I tolerate. Women were born to be bred and listen to and do what they are told. My father taught me that at a young age, and I still believe it today.

I tilt my head to the side, watching her closely. She clears her throat. "Mr. Blackwell?" The nurse asks as she quickly makes her way over to the counter next to me.

Her voice is soft, her confidence swaying a little, I am not surprised most women lose it when they get around me. I can't blame them. I am intimidating by nature. Both of my parents are lawyers and own and run their own firm, and, of course, they are the lawyers for the NHL.

Since my parents are wealthy and are working with one of the best teams, I get all the wealth and attention as well. I love attention and I love hockey, so it is a win - win for me.

I know most of the players and get invited to the private events and parties. I am living my best life at 32 years old. What woman wouldn't be nervous around me, right?

She turns around, grabbing tightly onto the counter as she looks over my face. It fucking hurts; I know I will have a black eye by tomorrow, but I have never been able to keep my mouth shut.

"What happened?" She asks as she pushes off of the counter, stopping in front of me. The ocean smell overwhelms me as she slowly lifts her left hand, gently touching the area around my eye.

She stops for a moment, our eyes locking. She is rapidly searching my eyes, looking for what I don't know, but this woman has my heart beating.

Strange.

"I got in a fight" I say softly, watching her every move, she drops her hand from my face, taking her warmth with her.

I want to feel her touch again.

No, I fucking need to feel it again.

"You will live. Put ice on the area," she says as she turns to grab the folder. I grab her wrist before she can. I quickly get off of the table and pull her against me.

Her eyes are wide, her breathing becoming a little unhinged.

"What is your name?" I ask and demand at the same time.

"Alexa," she answers.

I nod. "Brad."

A smile forms on her lips. "Can you let go of me, Brad?" She asks.

I take in a deep, shaky breath. I don't want to let go, but I will for now.

She turns and grabs my records as she stands up straight and looks at me for a moment. Then she nods, turns around, and makes her way to the door. She grabs the doorknob and my heart races as I close the distance between us, grabbing her elbow gently, or at least as gently as I can.

"Have dinner with me," I demand and ask.

"No."

"No," I repeat back.

Did she really just fucking say no to me? No woman has ever told me no.

She shakes her head, "No."

"Alexa, please have dinner with me," I say through gritted teeth, already losing my patience with my lack of control I have over this nurse.

"I don't do the dating thing," she says, pulling her elbow from me. Before I can say anything, she opens the door and walks out.

Leaving me stunned and pissed off.

She doesn't know who I am, but she is about to.

No one says no to Brad Blackwell, and certainly not a nobody nurse.

Chapter 3
Alexa

At the end of my fourteen hour shift, I am covered in blood, sweat, and vomit. I can smell myself, and it makes me want to gag. I took a quick shower in the locker room, but I can still smell it, even after changing into another set of scrubs. There are just some smells that just linger, and it just so happens vomit is definitely one of them.

I am finally walking out of the back doors of the hospital; it was a long shift. Whatever could go wrong went wrong. I need to get out of here before something else happens.

They all know I won't say no to extra shifts, or covering for someone, or staying after to help the doctors. Normally I would want that distraction, but now I need a different type of distraction.

My mind is racing, my anxiety is taking over. There are only a few things that can take this feeling away, and it's not another shift being covered in blood, sweat, and vomit.

I think I am just a magnet for bad luck. What sounds good right now is going out dancing and letting loose.

It is one of the main things I do that gets rid of my anxiety; if I don't do something, it will soon turn into a full-blown panic attack.

You would think I would go home and get some rest, like a normal person would. But my home is empty, not a home at all, just four walls of space. I don't think I have ever actually felt at home in any of the places I have lived.

I have always felt like an outsider looking in, someone who has been used, ignored, and pushed to the side. Someone that just couldn't live up to what my family wanted. They had an image to uphold, and as their only daughter, I have destroyed it on many fronts.

Which is why I left and moved. Everyone knew who I was because of my parents or because of the booze, parties, and the many sex partners I was going through.

Four years ago, my parents' name was dragged through the mud because of me, what happened to me, me being so careless that I allowed it to happen, or that is the way my mother put it.

I shake my head and take in a deep breath.

I will sleep once I can't walk from moving to the sounds, escaping. I won't drink. I have another shift in a few hours, which is why at the hospital we all sleep here and there when we can.

You can find not just doctors sleeping in the hallways on beds, but also us nurses. It is just part of the life; we all live and breathe the hospital.

After turning Brad down for dinner, the ER got even busier than it was before, and I couldn't get his voice out of my head. I know I shocked him by saying no. He doesn't look like the type of guy that women turn down.

But I am nothing special. In fact, I can't get many things right in my life. I am loud, stubborn; I freaking trip over air; I love frozen pizza, and I am normally lost in a book or writing when I am not at the hospital. I have my best friend, and that is about it.

My circle is small. My best friend saved me. She doesn't realize it, but when the darkness was drowning me, she was my lifejacket that kept me from fully drowning.

I take a deep breath as I make it to my car, unlock it and open the back door, quickly looking around at the practically empty parking lot. I quickly remove my dark purples scrubs and reach into my gym bag, grabbing the crop top and leggings.

I hear people laughing as I quickly strip and pull up my leggings and pull my crop top over my sports bra. I am not big about fancy clothing, if I could wear sweatpants I would. I love sweatshirts, and being comfy, but being a nurse, I don't think my patients would take me seriously. So I play the part the hospital wants me to play, but after I clock off, I let loose and get lost in my thoughts.

Which is why dancing is my cure right now. I can dance, maybe make out with a few strangers, then go home, eat and sleep, then get up and do it all over again.

After what happened four years ago, I am distant to most except for my bestie, and I do certain things in a certain order. I enjoy knowing what is going to happen in my life, but also the control.

That night four years ago changed me. I felt out of control and powerless, and since that night, I promised myself I would change and never put myself in that situation again, and so far, I have kept my promise to myself.

I quickly get out of my car and shut the door. The wind is blowing, but it is warm. I take in a deep breath of the fresh air. On the drive to the club, I sprayed my perfume. I can't smell the vomit anymore, and I hope that no one else can, either.

I love these leggings because one they make my ass look fantastic, but also on either side of my thighs, it has pockets. I place my phone in my left pocket and my debit card and keys in the other.

I have never been a purse type of girl; I enjoy being able to be free, plus my memory is not that good. I am always misplacing things, and me going into a club with a purse would probably not be a good thing. Even though I am not drinking, with my luck, I would end up with only my keys at the end of the night.

I make my way across the parking lot. I can hear the music thumping as I keep a tight hold on my ID. The line is leading all the way around the corner of the club. but luckily I have a pass. I come here enough; I bought the membership, yes you heard me right. I pay for a club membership.

I hate lines, and I am beyond impatient. The membership allows me not to lose my cool.

The bouncer nods at me and smiles. As he opens the door, I walk quickly past him, slapping his shoulder as I do.

Jimmy is a nice guy, a retired fighter, covered in tattoos. He is dominant when he needs to be but still has a sense of humor. I only know because when I started coming here, he looked so damn serious I had to crack a joke, and now it's our thing.

He will find me after a while and tell me a joke, and I will do the same. I know nothing else about him except that I trust I am safe with him around, which is a lot for me to say. I don't trust people, and men, well I have a hard time with them after what happened to me.

I am better now, but still, when I feel uncomfortable, I have no problem finding my way out and quickly. I slowly make my way through the crowd towards the bar. The music is blaring so loud it is making it hard to think straight, which is perfect.

I stop at the bar and wave, catching the bartender's attention. The bartender who just happens to be my best friend. She moved in with me; she wanted us to live together, but I hate feeling like I am a burden. She needs her own space, and she doesn't need someone that when they do sleep has nightmares, so instead of screaming throughout the night, I started taking medications that help with my PTSD symptoms, and so far, they are working.

So, I came here not only to dance and not think but also to ask my best friend if she will move in with me. Like I said before, my house is empty and doesn't feel like home, but with her there, I know the vibes would change.

She doesn't know it, but I need her like I need air; she is my strong foundation when I feel like I am going to fall through the cracks of my life. She will never let me fall, and I will never let her fall.

Natalie stops on the other side of the bar, leaning over the counter. I do the same as we try to hug each other the best we can. She pulls back and gives me a smile. I would die for this woman without a second thought.

"I have a request," I say over the music.

She tilts her head to the side, and her smile widens.

I chuckle and shake my head. "Move in with me, bestie."

Her smile fades, and her eyes fill with tears. I reach out my hands over the counter, and she takes them, not needing to think for one second.

"Of course, bestie," she says, not able to hide her excitement.

This is how it should have been all along, her and me against the world. I was just trying to protect her from me, but she is faithful, loyal, and fierce, and I know she needs me just as much as I need her.

"Thank you for being my strong foundation," I say, getting choked up by my few words.

"Thank you for being my person," she replies. We release our hold on each other's hand and quickly wipe away our tears.

We both chuckle, and she nods. That is her silent way of telling me to get out there.

It is time I let loose and I only have a few hours until once again I am covered in vomit, sweat, and blood.

I will get lost in the music, and for a short amount of time, the anxiety will be replaced with peace.

Chapter 4
Cole

Ipark the car, and everyone in the back seat gets out.

We had a really late practice on the ice. We are all the starting players, and the pressure is on us to stay that way. One wrong move, and our dreams can be taken away and shattered like ice.

We love what we do; it is why we do it, but the competition can be fierce, overwhelming, and intense. But it's worth it in the end.

I take in a deep breath as I continue to listen to the song; I don't know it, but it gets my mind off of all the things I know I did wrong during practice. I am the right defenseman, and Wright is the left. Our whole purpose is to protect our goalie like our lives depend on it.

There were a few times tonight that other players got past me, and they shouldn't have. I need to do better, be stronger, be faster. I need to make sure that no one, and I mean no one, can fucking get past me to get to my goalie.

Some nights, practice is great; others are like this one, where I am tired, worn down, and too hard on myself, but we all are. Everyone can tell us we are amazing and say that we got this, but every single one of us is only focusing on what we need to work on to get better.

Wright is a good player. He is strong, young, and determined beyond belief. He has had my back, and I have had his, but we still need to work on our communication skills. It isn't his fault; it is mine.

Communication has never been something I am good at it, growing up the way I did, and trying to survive has made me as cold as ice. Everything about me can be compared to the game I play, the game I love, the game that has saved my life.

I take in a deep shaking breath; I feel a hand squeeze my shoulder, my eyes open, I turn my head, locking eyes with my best friend. Kolby. He is a year older than me, and we have been in each other's lives for as long as I can remember, both of us working our way up through the league. Kolby is our goalie, and he is built for it, too.

Kolby, like me, is covered in tattoos and cut beyond belief, but he is bigger than me. He is a few inches taller than me and has to be stronger so he can take on the pain that is put on his body from being the goalie.

I have protected him from the opposing team, and I have also protected him when we were growing up. We were two kids trying to find a way out of the chaos and escape the life that was trying to kill us, and it almost did.

Unlike the other players on our team, we have a dark past. One that almost cost us our positions when the media found out who we were. The NHL almost turned on us, but our team and coaches made sure we weren't ripped apart.

"It's time to let loose, brother," Kolby says softly.

Even though he is older than me, I took on the abuse and pain for us both when we were younger; the streets weren't kind to two kids. We have both been in the gutter, on the streets, just waiting for trash to be thrown out so we could eat.

He is not my brother by blood, but he is my brother by choice. I would die for this man, and he would die for me, which is why protecting him on the ice comes so naturally. We are family, and nothing will ever change that.

I nod. He squeezes my shoulder again and smiles, opening the car door, and slides out. I turn off the car and do the same.

The warm breeze hits my skin, my jeans hug my muscles of my thighs, my button-up shirt hugs my chest and abs, and I slowly roll up the sleeves, right above my elbows.

Kolby comes up behind me grabbing onto my shoulders, forcing me to move forward towards the back entrance of the club.

A groan leaves me as he grabs the door and pulls it open. We both walk inside, the heavy door slamming behind us, making my anxiety intensify a bit. I hate small spaces; that hasn't changed from when I was a kid, and I don't think it ever will.

Kolby releases his hold on my shoulders and pushes past me. I turn and make my way through the crowd of people towards the bar. I know where Kolby is going, so I turn and watch him make his way over to the same bar stool he sits on, wanting and needing to talk to the bartender. He has it bad for her. I can't tell for sure on her side, but she flirts too.

Kolby has never had a problem getting women. In fact, they fall on their knees for him, but he doesn't pay attention to those women. They don't impress him;, he likes them sassy and cocky, and he found that in the bartender. She makes him work for everything.

It drives him crazy, and makes me laugh, he is so fucking whipped.

I lean against the counter as she makes her way over to me, setting the whisky in front of me. She gives me a smile and nod, as she turns and makes her way back down towards Kolby. He is leaning over the bar, watching her closely as she makes other drinks.

I shake my head and chuckle as I bring the glass up to my lips. I turn and look out at the dance floor, feeling my heart stop as the song switches to something up beat and sexual. My hand shakes with the glass as I lowering it to the counter as my eyes stay locked on the dance floor, or I should say locked on to the woman that is on the dance floor.

Her hips sway to the music, her tight leggings showing off her curves in all the right ways. Her crop top teasing me, showing off a little of her skin as she sways and lifts her hands, lifting the shirt along with them.

Fuck, holy fuck.

I clear my throat as she turns, taking my breath away. Her head lifted, falling back slightly, her eyes are closed as she allows the song to take her over.

Fuck, she is gorgeous. Breathtaking doesn't even describe what she is. The darkness of the club makes it hard to get a good read on her, but from what I can see, she has curves in all the right places; she isn't like the other women I have seen trying to get in my pants or throwing themselves at me. We call those women bunnies or groupies.

No, this woman, she has dark brown hair, it's up in a messy bun, her crop top hugs her upper body, showing off her amazing fucking boobs. Most men seem to like big boobs, but not me. This woman has the perfect size to fit into my hands.

Damn.

My mouth waters as my eyes scan down her front, her leggings hugging her thighs. The boots she is wearing come up to almost her knees. I look back up at her face; she isn't wearing much makeup from what I can see, but she doesn't need to.

She is naturally gorgeous. I can tell it is just who she is, and I am betting she doesn't even realize just how beautiful she is. She doesn't see how these men are looking at her. But I can see it. Her vibes take over the dance floor. Women are staring at her; men want to fuck her.

My cock presses against my jeans. I shift to relieve some of the pressure, forcing a groan to leave me as my cock pulses in my jeans. My eyes stay locked completely on her.

I am so fucked.

There are strangers all around her, dancing and laughing. I watch closely as a few men come up to her, boxing her in. My pulse races, and my eyes see nothing but red. I slap my hand down on the counter, watching as one of them grabs her hips and sways. Her body stills. I am not normally possessive or jealous of someone I don't know.

But this woman has already put me under a spell.

Tinker Bell has sprinkled her sparkling fairy dust on me.

I am cooked, slice me open and see me bleed. Which is exactly what I will do for this beautiful, breathtaking brunette. If anyone is watching me like I am watching her, I look like a freaking stalker. But I don't care at this moment. I don't care that I have been staring at her for so long with my mouth open that my tongue is dry. That it's hard for me to breathe, and it's not because of the crowded bar, it is because of her.

Damn me to hell, I am going to jail tonight. I will be sleeping next to Joe, the hairy scary in a cell that is not made for two grown men. He will snore, and I will get no sleep as I wait for my best friend to bail me out.

I quickly stand up straight, but before I can start to move through the crowd of strangers, she is already turning around and placing her hands on his chest, giving him a shove back.

I hate she touched him at all. I hate the fact that those three men think and believe that she is available to do so.

All three of the men laugh and shake their heads as she places her hands on her hips. Sassy little thing.

A smirk forms across my lips as the men walk away. She stands still, watching them leave, and when the song changes and lowers her hands to her sides, and slowly starts moving again. My cock pulses again as I quickly make my way through the crowd. As I come up behind her, the smell of the ocean hitting my nose.

I inhale deeply, taking in her scent as I stop behind her. She stills again and turns, but I grab her hips, forcing her to stay where she is. I lean down, resting my lips against her ear.

"Get lost with me, baby girl," I whisper, feeling my heart race against her back.

She doesn't respond. Instead, she lifts her arms, placing her hands on the back of my head and neck, and sways. I take in a deep breath of her scent, wanting to fucking bathe it in.

Chapter 5
Alexa

I don't know how many songs me and this stranger have been dancing to, but my body is covered in sweat, and my pussy has been pulsing since he whispered in my ear. His voice was gentle and dominate, a perfect mixture that caused my pussy to purr for him.

Oh fuck. Purr? Really Alexa. My best friend says I am like a cat. Loyal to a fault, but distant. Loving and kind, but can go off when I feel uncomfortable or threatened. If I am a cat, she is like a German Shepard: loyal, loving, kind, and also very protective.

We go together like two peas and a pod.

I try to focus on his body against mine, instead of my imploding thoughts that will lead nowhere. I can't think straight, which I know was the point, but now all I can think about is his cock stretching my pussy, making me moan.

No Alexa, be a good girl, and stay clear, stay far away.

No cock, no stretching pussy, no. N.O. spells no.

His scent consumes me, taking me away from the chaos inside my head to a deep forest. He smells like pine trees. It's a comforting smell, something that makes me forget we are in a club, getting lost in each other.

The words he whispered to me echo inside me. I was ready to turn around and give him a piece of my mind, but as soon as he whispered those words to me, I melted. I couldn't force him away, not when everything inside me was screaming at me to latch on and never let go.

I can feel his hard cock against my back as we continue to sway, his warm breath on my neck sending goosebumps throughout my body. I can tell he is some kind of athlete; I don't care what kind. In this town, men come from all over to train and get ready.

His hard muscles trap me, his smell imprisons me in the best possible way. Nothing will happen tonight, nothing at all, except this. I can escape with him, get lost in him, even if it's only for tonight.

I promised myself no relationships, no sex, no closeness. I have to keep my promise. Because if I don't, I know I won't survive myself or the men that will come knocking at my door.

I am an addict in every sense of the word for instant gratification, and sex is the best way to get it. My parents don't understand why I am the way I am, and I don't understand why they just can't open their eyes and see that I didn't want to be this way, reckless and impulsive, but I can't escape what that man did to me. I can't escape the fact that family is supposed to protect family, and my parents didn't.

They didn't believe me. All they ever cared about was their image. They didn't care what I wanted or needed, they never even asked. I wanted a career in writing; they told me I would never make it. My father and mother chose my degree and what school, and even applied for me.

They acted as if nothing happened to me. Everyone, I guess, deals with trauma in different ways, and I just do it in a "I am going to drink until I black out, not say no to any man" kind of way.

Then when I did say no, it didn't matter, because I had been painted as a sinful whore.

My parents didn't say it, but I know they breathed better once I left for college, more like they forced me out and didn't give me a choice.

The song comes to an end and my stomach twists into an unsettled knot as I'm pulled from the past. I drop my hands from the stranger and he loosens his grip on my hips, allowing me to turn around. I look up and my heart stops.

His eyes rapidly search mine. He looks like a lost puppy, one that wants to be held and loved, but also scared and distant. His deep blue eyes are pulling me in, making me want to drown in them.

The lights turn on, forcing me out of the trance. I break my eyes from him. As I look around the club, everyone is leaving the dance floor, grabbing their things and heading towards the exits.

My attention snapped back to the gorgeous stranger in front of me, and I place my hands on his chest. I slowly popped up on my tippy toes, placed a chaste kiss on his cheek and quickly pull back. His eyes instantly filled with passion, concern, worry, and fire. A mixture that both confuses and intrigues me.

I lower my hands from his chest and take in a deep breath. "Thank you for getting lost with me," I whisper.

He nods, a small smile forms across his lips, I lick mine, imagining what his lips would taste like.

Chastity Belt. That is what I am going to buy off of Amazon as soon as I get into my car, and I am giving the key to my bestie. She will hide it far, far away from me.

I go to take a step back, but his hands on my hips tighten, keeping me in place. My heart is racing.

"We can't do this." I confess in a firm voice. I don't know if the firmness is for him or for me.

"Do what?" He asks tilting his head to the side, giving me those puppy dog eyes.

Oh, my lanta.

A chuckle leaves me. "This," I motion between us.

"Why?" He asks confused.

"Because I am not good, and you need to focus on whatever sport you play," I say, folding my arms over my chest.

His smile widens. "What makes you think I am an athlete?"

"The muscles, thick thighs, gorgeous smile, and the shiner underneath your right eye," I say, gesturing at his face.

He shakes his head and laughs. "Mhmm."

Oh turkey bagel. The Mhmm thing.

Really?

"I'm a nurse," I confess. Needing him to stop looking at me like I am a treat he wants to devour for the rest of his life.

He nods, his smile slowly fading.

"I have to go," I whisper, pulling back.

He releases his grip. I look over his shoulder at my best friend. Her eyes are deadlocked on me, her eyebrows going up and down.

Oh boy.

I shake my head and look up at the man that helped me get lost. I am in such big trouble. If I stay any longer, I know my tongue will be in his mouth within minutes.

My breath is shaky as I walk around him and head straight towards the back exit.

The best thing for the both of us, is to forget about this, forget everything.

I am not going down this road, yet again.

Nope not happening.

Chapter 6
Brad

I sit back and take a deep breath while I squeeze the steering wheel. Here I sit, waiting for her to get home, and I hate waiting. I am not a patient man. When I want something or in this case someone, I get it.

My mind has been racing since she turned me down. I was shocked and almost lost my shit in that damn hospital. Fortunately, I kept my cool. I can't draw too much attention to myself. I have an image to uphold. My family's name is important, and I won't risk the wrath of my father. Even though I am a grown ass fucking man, he still scares the shit out of me.

I have gone over it time and time again inside my head, and it just doesn't make any sense. The encounter with her was on point. I had game; I know I did. But she still brushed me off as if I was just another patient.

Women throw themselves at me, beg me, want to please me. But not her. Alexa acts as if I am just some other guy. I am not. I never have been. I don't understand her logic. It is a privilege to be with me. I can open up so many doors for her, and I can promise she has never had a cock like mine.

Fuck.

She is driving me crazy. I don't know her. I don't really fucking want her, but I want to play with her because she doesn't want me. Does that make fucking sense to you?

It doesn't to me and, in fact, it is just making me fucking spin more.

I followed her after work, and I hoped she would go home, but fuck no, she had to go to a club.

I saw her at the club. I saw her, but she didn't see me. She was too busy getting lost in some fuck tard to pay attention to people around her. She blew me off, said no to going on a date with me, and went to a club instead?

She rather dance with some stranger than go out with me?

A dark chuckle leaves me as I shake my head. I can get anyone I want, and this woman thinks she is better than me. She thinks she can just turn me down, make a fool out of me and I will what…just let it stand?

She should be grateful that I am even interested at all. Maybe it is the chase, maybe it is because she isn't throwing herself at me. Whatever it is, I want her, and I want to see her on her knees, begging for my cock, just like every other whore has.

She isn't special by any means. Her hair needs some work, she would look a lot better with makeup, her wearing contacts instead of glasses would help, and her clothes. She needs to wear something that is more I don't know, fitting? At the club, she was wearing a crop top and leggings, which looked good on her, but not great.

She would look better if her body was more toned, and I can tell she doesn't care what she puts in her body. But lucky for her, I know what I like, what I want, and I can help guide her, after all that is what she needs a strong man to guide her and make decisions for her, because when she is left to make her own, she looks like she does now.

I saw fucking red when I saw that man touch her. He looks familiar, but I can't figure out from where. But watching him dance with her, whispering in her ear; it took everything I had not to go over there and rip his fucking head off.

She isn't mine yet, but she will be and when she is, her entire world is going to change. It will change in the best way possible. She will be my good little slut and do as she is told.

Chapter 7
Cole

For the life of me, I can't get that woman out of my head. She took over my dreams. Dreams of her pussy wrapped tightly around my cock and moaning my name. I have woken up with boners before, but not like this morning.

I had to stay in the shower for thirty extra damn minutes. There was no way I was going to come to practice with a full-on squash pushing against my sweatpants.

Kolby would never, ever let me live it down.

I sit back on the bench and place my phone in my bag. I found her on TikTok and other social media platforms this morning. I have been going through them obsessively. She hasn't posted anything in the last few months, and it makes me wonder what she has been through, makes me curious of why she said she would be bad for me.

She doesn't realize that it is the other way around. I am obsessive, possessive, and unhinged. I wear my emotions on my sleeve, and I have been told I have a temper. Which has been good for my position, but not so much with relationships.

If I am not careful, I will give her the "stranger danger" vibes, and I don't want that. But I can't stop myself from looking at her pictures, reading her words.

Her pain is like my pain. We are bonded by pain. She just doesn't know it yet.

Fuck, I am giving myself "stranger danger" vibes.

Dear Lord.

I take in a deep breath as the guys pat my shoulder as they head onto the ice.

I shake my head and stand stretching; every part of my body is screaming for me to go out on the ice. This is what I live for. So why the flying donkey hell do I feel like that is about to change?

I skate onto the ice, pulling my gloves on, and holding tightly onto my helmet as I make my way to my spot. I need to focus on practice, but the only thing I can focus on is the way it felt to have that beautiful brunette in my arms.

Her scent, the ocean soothing scent, still lingers on my clothes. I close my eyes for a moment, as I allow her words to echo inside my mind. She is sassy and guarded, but I could see it in her eyes. She wants me.

Even if her mind and heart are telling her to run, her body is betraying her.

She fit so perfectly in my arms, like she was made to be there. I hate the idea of not knowing anything about her, and I hate the idea that I am here, and she is wherever the hell she is right now.

"Bro" Kolby yells, getting my attention.

Right, practice, teamwork. Fuckkkk.

Kolby is already at the goalie, and Wright is pulling his helmet over his head.

The scouts will be at the next home game, which is in six months. That gives us just enough time to tighten our communication and get our shit fine tuned.

Wright has wanted to go to the Olympics since I have known him. He has big dreams for a young guy, and I will do everything I can to help him achieve them.

Kolby and I don't plan to go anywhere. This is the team we plan on retiring from. Plus, being in this town allowed me to give my birth mom a better life, and get her the hell away from the men who refused to let her go, away from the life that refused to let her go.

When I was younger, I didn't understand where she went, or why she couldn't be with me. I thought she didn't want me, but now I understand.

My birth mom has an issue with addiction, not only substances but also abusive men. She gave me up to save me. It wasn't her fault I went to the streets and got into the trouble I did.

Hockey saved me, and now it is my turn to save my mom. I paid for her six months of rehab, and she stayed a full year, so while me and the boys are getting ready for the scouts, she is working on herself.

Today I get to go visit her, and of course, Kolby wanted to go as well. We will go right after practice.

It wasn't hard for me to forgive her. We all have a past, and we all deal with pain in different ways. Me hating my mom won't change what happened to her or me. So, I am going to be a good son now and show her that my forgiveness is real.

I see the shame and guilt in her eyes when I come and see her, and I am hoping that one day her shame and guilt will be replaced with love and joy.

"Jackson, get your head in the game," coach yells at me, knocking me back to reality.

I take a deep breath and pull down my helmet. I hunch over, banging my stick against the ice, locking eyes with my teammates across the ice. My heart begins to pound for a completely different reason now.

Boner gone. Primal mode to rip my teammates apart, activated.

Chapter 8
Alexa

I shut my car door, and grab my bags and coffee, once again heading towards the doors that will take all of my energy away once again. I can never catch up, it seems like, never enough sleep, never enough coffee, never enough hours in the day. It will never be enough.

I look down at my phone as I walk across the parking lot, and scroll through my messages from my parents. Same old, same old. They tell me to stay in line, and to be a good daughter.

Good daughter, like I am bad or something. It makes my stomach twist into an uncomfortable knot. My heart sinks, as there is no love in their messages, only distance, always distance.

"Alexa," a dark deep voice calls out, causing me to scream, run into the entrance doors, and there goes my coffee, right in my face, and down my scrubs.

"Son of a donkey," I growl.

I hear a chuckle as I quickly turn around and see Brad standing a foot away from me. His eyes filled with laughter as he bites his bottom lip, trying not to laugh.

Tears fill my eyes, but I suck them back, bad luck.

"Are you okay?" He asks, with only a little bit of concern in his eyes. He is dressed in a black suit, his hair held back with man gel or whatever it is called, his jawline is sharp, and his swimmer body showing through even with a suit on.

He reminds me of one of those models on a billboard. The kind that makes you almost hit the car in front of you as you are trying to figure out exactly what he is trying to sell you.

It is him, or it is the jeans. No one really knows.

"Do I look okay to you?" I snap.

I am not a people person never have been, which is funny because I have to be for my job. But, right now, I am not on the clocked, so forced, happy face Alexa is not out to play along right now.

I hate mornings, so freaking much.

"No," he says, shaking his head.

"Seems you already know the answer to your question, sir." I say in an irritated tone, as I slightly turn and swipe my badge against the little grey box. The light goes from red to green, the door lock pulls back, and the doors open wide for me.

Man, I really wanted this coffee. Like really really badly. Now my scrubs get the caffeine and I get nothing.

I take in a breath as I make my way through the open doors. Before I can make it very far, Brad has my arm in his hand, keeping me in place.

A groan escapes my lips as he tightens his grip and moves in front of me, blocking my way deeper into the ER. I lock eyes with him. He is calm and amused, but I am neither. I just want to go one day without wearing the liquid that is supposed to go down my throat and give me energy.

That would be great…that would be a good day. A win in my book for sure. Today, though, is not that freaking day.

"Brad, what are you doing here?" I ask, just needing him to go away.

He doesn't respond at first. I watch his mouth open and close, knowing he wants to say something but my irritation is growing with the passing silence between us.

I don't have time for this.

I go to walk around him, but he walks into me and tightens his grip. My heart races with the contact, his scent surrounding me.

"I need a check-up," he says calmly.

I can't help it. A laugh leaves me, but it is more like a sob laugh.

"What? You don't need a checkup. I can see the shiner is healing just fine," I say, motioning towards his eye.

"Well, maybe I got into another fight," he says, amused.

I roll my eyes and raise my eyebrows at him, looking over his face, and back up to his eyes.

"Okay, maybe I haven't, but you never know there might be underlying damage," he confesses.

"Oh, really?"

"Yes! You see, when I look at this girl, her beauty blinded my vision," he says with a serious face.

I roll my eyes again, not being able to stop myself. Holy fuck, really?

"Really?" I say trying to keep back my laugh.

He nods like a bobble head that has just taken a line of crack, or the toy is broken.

My laughter gets louder at his cheesy line and my funny thought. My eyes roll for the third time so much, I probably look like my eyes are popping out of my head. "That sounds like a you problem, sir."

"I think you can help cure me though," he says with confidence, making me stiffen.

One thing I have learned about men, about people in general is everyone has motives and intentions. We all want something. So what does this man want?

"How so?"

"Go to dinner with me," he blurts out.

I tilt my head to the side as I keep my eyes on him. There is humor, desperation, and passion in his eyes.

It is just dinner Alexa, just dinner.

"If I say yes, will you stop with the cheesy lines?" I ask.

He nods, a smirk forming across his lips.

I let out an irritated but amused breath. "Fine, just dinner."

His smirk forms into a full-blown smile.

"Pick me up out front at 1 a.m."

"I'll be here," he says with confidence.

He wants to go to dinner, fine. I will be hungry and I will need to eat. It might be dinner, but it doesn't have to be a date. The bar will do just fine.

He leans in, kissing my cheek and letting go of my arm.

"I will see you later, babes," he says with amusement.

My brows raise again.

"I have to go change. Someone made me wear my coffee," I half grumble.

He reaches out his hand with a nice warm coffee, and without thinking, I grab it. I am greedy and I need this more than he does, plus he cost me my coffee.

"Truce?" He asks.

"For now," I reply, taking a sip of the deliciousness. My eyes fall closed and an almost moan slips past my lips.

"Fuck," he whispers as he walks around me. I can feel his presence leave as I open my eyes, but I refuse to turn around and watch him leave.

Man, I hope I don't regret this.

Chapter 9
Brad

I lean against my car and pull out my phone. I am a very impatient man, or that is what I have been told, anyway. There is nothing wrong with wanting things in a certain amount of time. Time frames are important. Waiting for this woman to get off her shift is annoying, but I will wait because I need to at least taste her. I need to know if my obsession is placed for good reason.

Is it the chase I am after because she doesn't throw herself at me, or is it because her sweet pussy will be worth it?

I don't want to wait much longer to find out. I need to know if I need to move on to the other women on my phone, or if this nurse is worth my time.

I swipe the screen and push on the icon for my messages. I scroll through the many messages from women, and, of course, my parents.

The pressure is on to make sure everything is in place. Everything has to be perfect because my father will accept nothing less. I don't know how to fail; it isn't an option for me.

Everything has an order, its rightful place, and I freak out when things don't go the way I have envisioned inside my head. I don't enjoy feeling out of control. I buckle down and make damn sure everything goes my way, and if it starts to stray, I bend it to my will.

Just like I am doing with Alexa, she won't escape me. My father taught me at a young age, the only way to control a woman and keep her in line is to dig your claws in her so deep that she doesn't know how to live without you.

That is my plan with this sassy nurse. Her job is going to be a problem, but I will deal with that later.

I click on the first message from a chick I fucked a few days ago. My screen fills with her naked pictures. Damn, she is fine, but her body could use some work, but she does have the curves in all the right places.

I have strict standards for who is with me. My image is important. I look good, so, of course, the girl on my arm has to look good as well. Their appearance reflects on me.

I look up from my phone when I hear the doors open. Alexa is in leggings and a white crop top. Damn, she is fucking hot. Her hair is in a messy bun, and she is holding her bags.

What is in those bags?

I don't know.

I shake my head as I put my phone in my pocket and push off of my car. Opening the side door for her, she stops in front of me. She looks tired and needs coffee, cock, and food, and I plan on giving all three to her. That is, if she lets me, but if she doesn't, I will just amp up my charm and she will cave. They all do.

"Long day?" I ask as she slides into my car.

She groans, making me chuckle. She is cute, I will give her that. She is sassy; I like it.

"Yes," she says softly as I close the door and make my way around the front of my car, opening my door and sliding inside.

"Where too, babes?" I ask with hope in my voice.

Her brows raise for a moment. "The bar."

We could go anywhere, and that is where she wants to eat, yeah that will be changing. I will add it to my growing list for her.

I reach out my hand, resting it on her leg. She slowly moves away. I take my hand back and hold tightly onto the steering wheel as I speed out of the parking lot, towards the bar down the street.

The silent trip from the hospital to the bar seems like it took an eternity, even though in reality it was only a few minutes. She just stared out of the window, with her hands resting in her lap. I wanted to take her hand in mine, but getting rejected again was not high on my list.

Anger boils inside my chest as I pull into the parking lot and turn off my car. I open my door and she takes a deep breath, as if it is a chore to be with me right now.

This woman is going to make me see red without saying a goddamn word.

She opens her door and gets out, closing the door behind her. She wraps her arms tightly around herself as I get out and catch up to her. I can hear the music blasting from the club side as we head into the restaurant entrance. The restaurant is not as packed as the club side, thank fuck.

I follow behind her, gently placing my hand on her lower back as we find a seat in the middle of the room. She takes a seat and I do the same, and then she picks up the menu, acting as if I am just some other person she is with.

"You, okay?" I ask, picking up my menu while I watch her closely.

She lowers the menu and locks eyes with me.

"Yeah?" Is the only word she says as she looks back at the menu.

I mumble words I can't even understand underneath my breath just as the waitress comes to the table to take our order. I look up at her, and she blushes, glances at Alexa and then turns back to me fuck me eyes.

"Know what you want, baby?" She asks, her voice low and sultry.

I look at Alexa, and she is looking at the waitress, but there isn't a hint of jealousy on her face. The smirk on my face falls as I look at the woman next to me.

"Burger, and a vodka soda, and my date here will have a salad and water," I order, looking at Alexa.

Now there is anger written all over her face.

"Actually, I will have the burger and a diet soda, please," she disobeys, looking at me.

I don't break my eyes from hers as the woman walks away to place our order.

"I can order my own food," she says, annoyed.

"I know, but I just thought." I stop talking when she lifts her hand and shakes her head at me.

"Careful, Alexa," I warn in a low voice.

She leans forward. "Why?"

"I don't like being disrespected. Don't make me punish you," I warn.

A chuckle leaves her.

"Don't you find it disrespectful to order for someone you don't know?" She says, looking me up and down.

"Correction, someone I am getting know," I say through gritted teeth.

Deep breaths, Brad, deep breaths.

She nods.

"Sorry, let's start over, okay?" I implore her.

She thinks about it for a moment and nods, sitting back in her seat.

Jesus, fuck, this girl is going to be the death of me. I have already put my foot in my mouth and we've barely sat down. My normal charm will not get this girl. I need to switch it up before she walks out on me. And I will definitely have to punish her for doing that.

Chapter 10
Cole

Sweat covers my face and body as I lean forward on the bench in the middle of the locker-room. I rest my elbows on my legs as I take a deep breath, trying to get more air into my lungs.

Practice was brutal, but it is supposed to be that way. If my body didn't feel this way, I would be disappointed in myself. My muscles need to burn, my lungs need to struggle for air, and my mind needs to be racing with all the things I should have done better. The work is never done when you are a pro athlete, and when you are in the NHL, the pressure is on to be the best or you get replaced.

We all have to be at our best 24/7, or the dream gets taken away. I am do this because I love the sport, but I am also doing this so I can give my mom and me a better life.

I forgave my mother as soon as I knew the truth about why she was the way she was, why she gave me away. My mother was and is addicted to alcohol and cocaine. I don't know which one came first, but I know they almost permanently took her from me.

My mother needed to get money to support her habit, so she did what she was taught to do, and that was to use her body. I don't know who my father is, but I can only guess where he is now, either dead or in prison.

When I was younger, I asked her what his name was, and she looked at me with tears in her eyes. She whispered she didn't know before she leaned forward and I watched as she did a line off the coffee table. I went back to watching whatever movie she had put on for me, thinking it would shield me from what she was really doing.

When I was seven years old, she gave me up to the state, telling them I deserved better. The thought was loving, but the aftermath was dark. I bounced from foster home to foster home until I eventually ran away and met Kolby.

We became quick friends and stayed together. The path of self sabotage and destruction started from there. I could have sworn off drugs, drinking and women, and be a productive member of society, but I gave into the darkness. My mother said she wanted to give me a better life, but the real truth is I didn't stand a chance because I made the choice to destroy myself.

It was never her fault. Yes, she played some sort of rule, but I am a firm believer in that we make choices and those choices have consequences. I knew if Kolby and I didn't get out of the life, that we would both die or go to prison or both, it was just a matter of which one would happen first.

When we were fourteen, we were in one of the boy shelters and some NHL players came by to teach us about hockey. They said it was a good outlet for anger and trauma. I didn't realize how true his words would become until I got out on the ice and slammed into another kid to get the puck for the first time, and I did not get arrested. It became my new fucking addiction, my new escape, and the rest was history from there.

My heart is racing, as my friend squeezes my shoulder when he walks by. I need to do something, anything, to get these thoughts out of my head, but I guess the joke is on me. There is no escaping the darkness within. It's not like I can run from myself. Believe me, I have tried.

My phone buzzes, getting my attention. I reach down and grab it from my bag, seeing my mom's name across the screen. She has been doing so good that the rehab let her have her phone during certain times throughout the day. I take a deep, shaking breath before I swipe across the screen and click on her message.

I love you, son.

I love you too, mom.

I am doing as I am told this time, I promise.

I hope so.

I can see she reads it, but she doesn't reply. If I was her, I wouldn't either. She is trying; I know that, but my fear of losing her again to men and her substance of choice makes chills go down my spine.

I have forgiven her...truly I have. But that doesn't take away the sinking feeling that she will never truly give up her addictions. I can't blame her, not with the life she was given.

I am determined to be a better man, a better son, a better best friend. I will give her and those I love a better life, even if it means sacrificing myself to do it.

After all, when you are on the ice, you have to give your everything in order to be the star. I will do it. I will make it. I will not shatter like the ice I skate on.

Chapter 11
Natalie
1st Month

I sit back on my bed and scroll through TikTok while I half-heartedly listen to my bestie talking to her boyfriend…that is not really her boyfriend.

She is confused. I am confused; we are all fucking confused. Brad seemed nice at first, and still does at moments, but I can also see that there is something hidden underneath. Something that he doesn't want anyone to see.

I hear Alexa say goodbye, and I sit up and look over at my open door. She comes in and plops down on my bed, and I toss my phone to the side so I can lie down next to her, both of us looking up at the ceiling.

"How is prince charming?" I ask, turning to look at my best friend.

She inhales deeply as she turns her head and locks eyes with me. If I could take away all the pain that my best friend is feeling right now, I would.

Instead of answering my question, she asks. "If you could change my hair color, what would you change it to bestie?"

"What do you mean?" I ask, rapidly searching her eyes.

"I mean, if you could choose any color to change my hair, what color would you pick?" She asks softly. My heart races with her question, but also aches.

"You are perfect bestie. Why are you asking this?" I ask.

"Just curious," she says calmly.

"Did lover boy say something to you?" I ask, trying to hide the bitterness in my voice. But I have never been able to hide anything from my best friend.

She takes in a deep, shaky breath and turns her head away from me.

"Kinda, maybe, just suggested," she says.

"You do what is best for you, bestie. I think you are gorgeous." I tell her.

"Thank you," she says as she sits up and gets off of the bed. She makes her way over to the door and stops for a moment. I jump up and make my way over to her, grabbing her shoulders and squeezing.

"Why don't I make pizza and we can listen to music and read together," I suggest, in a hopeful voice. I just want to fix this, whatever this is.

"That sounds amazing," she replies with hope in her voice.

"It is a date," I say with a smile.

She chuckles and walks out of my room. I hate she is questioning her beauty and that lover boy or fuck nut, whatever you want to call him, seems to think he can put his nose where it doesn't belong.

I will protect her, from anyone, even him, even love, even if it means I have to take the bullets for her. I will always put her best interest first, and I don't think lover boy Brad can say the same.

Cole

Kolby pulls up into the same parking spot that he has parked in since we started coming here. You would think that after a certain amount of time of going somewhere, that the anxiety would go away, but it hasn't. It is very much still here.

Nothing seems to make it go away. I hate coming to places like this. I can see and hear the sickness. I know

I need to have a positive attitude for her, but sometimes it is hard to find.

My mom has asked me several times to come, and for the first few months, I refused to do so. Not because I didn't want to see her, but because I had to make sure she was being honest; that she was taking this seriously and that her words meant something this time.

I love my mom, but even now, as a grown ass man, when she messes up, it still stings. I lean my head against the headrest for a moment.

"You ready for this, man?" Kolby asks, pulling me from my thoughts.

"As ready as I will ever be," I confess.

Kolby and I get out of the car and make our way towards the entrance. I didn't want to come by myself. Hell, if I am being completely honest, I didn't want to come at all, but not because I don't want to see my mother. It is because I don't want anyone to know where she is.

I have learned over the last few years that the media will use whatever they can against me. I am a public figure, and that means nothing is off limits.

I have to protect my mom. The outside world would not understand her, and they would try to use her against me or me against her.

I will protect her, just like I will protect anyone else I love and care about.

I would die for my mother, just like I would die for Kolby.

It's what you do for family.

Chapter 12
Alexa

It has been about a month since I said went to dinner with Brad, and now he is everywhere. Every text is from him, every knock on my door is from him. He has been coming around so much that even my bestie has made a comment about his presence.

I just tell myself that it is because he likes me a lot, and I do like him, right?

Brad doesn't take no for an answer, that much he has shown me. He doesn't like that word, and the more time I spend with him, it is getting harder and harder to do so.

I make my way into the bathroom, stop in front of the mirror, and look at myself. It takes everything inside me not to flinch away from what I see looking back at me.

I have never liked what I see when I look in the mirror. It has been something I have battled for as long as I can remember, but lately it seems to be a lot worse. I am confident in who I am, but that doesn't mean I am confident in what I see.

I am nothing special, not really. My skin is flawless, but everything else about me is flawed. Let that set in for a minute.

I shake my head as I run my hands up and down my sides. All I see are the things I need to change and work on. My boobs are small, and my figure is not what it needs to be. I have curves, but I also have fat that covers me. I could be more toned, more fit in my stomach area.

I rest my hands against my bloated stomach. I crunch my nose as I look over my face, my glasses taking up most of my face. I don't know why but I have always liked the enlarged glasses.

I grab tightly onto the edge of the sink as I lower my head and try to fill my lungs with enough air that it will take away this feeling of spiraling.

The memory floods me, hitting me like a sack of bricks. Damn, here we go again.

"You're such a good girl. Now, keep quiet, you don't want them to hear us," he whispers into my ear, as his hand continues to move between my legs. My stomach tightens as tears fill my eyes.

"I don't want them to take you from me. You're my girl, right, Alex?" He asks eagerly.

I don't respond; I don't move; I do nothing. What can I do?

My knees give out as I loosen my grip on the sink and I fall to my knees. I am hyperventilating as I rest my forehead against the cool tile. These memories, memories I wish I could forget, continue to haunt me.

I hate I can't control when they come, but even more than the memories, I hate I can't control how my body reacts to them. It's as if I am right there all over again, helpless, hopeless and trapped in a situation I never wanted, but couldn't escape.

No one wants to hear about things like this, and that is why I let men use me, or at least I used to. It forced me to feel something, anything, but it has created this endless loop of trauma that I can't escape. Even in a new town, new house, new job, and now almost new man, or man that is trying to be my man, I still am struggling to keep it together.

This is bullshit muffins.

My breath is unsteady as tears fill my eyes. I refuse to let them fall as I slowly stand and turn, walking into the shower. I turn the water on as high as it will go and rest my hands against the tile as I lean into the running water. It burns my skin, but I don't scare.

The pain never lies. It is the gooey, ga ga emotions I can't rely on.

I wish the water could wash away how gross I feel right now. It has been years since he touched me, since he tainted me and created me into this person, but it still feels as if his fingers are still touching me.

"Bestie," Natalie yells, snapping me out of my head.

"I'm in the shower," I yell back as I stand up straight and run my hands through my now wet hair.

"He is at the door," she says as knocks at the door, making me jump.

"You scared the hell out of me," I holler as I turn around and grab the shampoo.

"He is a needy thing, isn't he?" She questions.

"Yeah, I guess," I say calmly, even though my heart is racing.

"I'll tell him you are busy. It's bestie day so he can wait," she says calmly, but I can hear the protectiveness in her tone.

Brad is cute, and charming, but also has secrets. I can see them, I just can't put my finger on what they are. He seems to be holding back, but maybe he is doing that because that is exactly what I am doing.

He has sides to him, personalities you could say, that throw me off; like when he tried to order for me at the restaurant. It is confusing. He acts as if he is right on the edge of losing control, and it scares me at times. But his good looks and sweetness has me forgetting about that fear. Like a fire that is mixed with sweet tasting honey.

I am losing my mind; that's what's happening.

I am prepared to run; I am always prepared to run. We haven't had the talk, the us talk, the are we together talk. I don't want to have that talk, and I don't want to put a label on what we are because then it will make it real. But Brad doesn't seem like the type of guy that will just let me be and not have a label. He seems to think or believe that our image is important, and has said as much many times over the last month. He makes comments about my hair and clothing, not in a rude way, but more in an *"I want to help you change and grow and be better"* kind of way.

We haven't even been intimate yet, although he has tried, but I always stop it before things go to far. I can see it annoys him, but he keeps coming back.

I let out my breath, as I rinse my hair, and turn off the water. I grab the towel from the wall and step out, wrapping it tightly around the body that I wish I could get out of.

"He's gone," she says calmly. I turn and look at her. Her eyes are locked on me, concern written all over her face.

"What's wrong?" I ask.

"He told me to remind you about your hair appointment," she replies.

"Oh, fuck," I whisper. I forgot he set that up for me a few days ago.

It took a few weeks, but he finally convinced me that maybe my confidence with my appearance would go up if I tried a different hair color. Maybe, just maybe, he is right.

"What?" She asks, putting her hands on her hips, making me chuckle and shake my head.

"He set up a hair appointment for me. I think it is time for a change." I say as I start to dry my hair.

"You mean he thinks it's time for a change?" She snarks.

I shake my head, "He suggested, and I agreed bestie."

"You are beautiful just the way you are, you know that, right?" She says as she walks up beside me.

"You have to say that. You are my best friend."

"I would tell you if I thought otherwise. You know I am not scared to tell you something," she says softly.

"I know. It's not a big deal, okay?"

"If you say so, just know I love you," she says, smiling at me.

"I love you too. I will be ready to leave in just a few minutes, okay?"

She nods and smiles, turning around and exiting the bathroom. I can't tell you how badly I need a bestie day.

She is the only one that has stayed by my side through everything, and I have done the same for her. We are two peas in a pod. She is my north star.

I turn and take a look in the mirror. A change wouldn't hurt.

Chapter 13
Cole

Islam my stick against the ice and glance at the timer.
It is down to thirty seconds. Thirty seconds until the buzzer goes off.

My heart races as I watch my best friend guard the goal. He is as determined as I am. It will go in, it fucking has to go in.

"Come on, Jackson," Coach yells as I take off down the ice, going back and forth, moving my stick, keeping the puck in the exact right spot to keep control.

I skate across the rink towards Kolby. He lowers himself, waiting to see what I am going to do next. He knows me well, but he doesn't know everything. I stop and go right, hitting the puck, a scream leaving my lips. I watch the puck fly across the ice. I hold my breath as I watch the puck go between his legs. Kolby falls to his knees, his chest heaving.

Coach is screaming and cheering. I look at my best friend, seeing a smile form across his lips. Even through his helmet, I can see it in his eyes. He nods and quickly gets up, skating towards me. He hugs me, his energy radiating off of him in waves.

My game is getting better, and Kolby is learning what to watch out for with the teams we will play against. The big game is in five months and until then every game will be a test of not just our skills as single players, but a test as a team.

We rise and fall as one.

"I'm proud of you," I say as Kolby lets me go.

He nods again. Even though he didn't block my shot, I learned that my strength has improved. If he can't stop my puck, it means I am learning and growing as a player, and right now that means everything.

I slowly take off my helmet and turn to skate towards the bench. I take a seat and hunch over, trying to catch my breath. Treating each practice like a game helps to keep me on track, but it isn't helping me to take my mind off of the woman who took my breath away that night in the bar.

I have gone back several times just praying she would be there, but she hasn't been. I am losing hope, but I am determined not to give up. I need to feel that possessive, primal need to have her against my body again. It is better than any substance, any practice, or any game I have experienced.

The rush of dopamine that went through me that night is not like anything I have ever felt before. I need it again; I need to touch her again, smell her again, to feel her again. I need to whisper things into her ear, feeling her body's need for me.

I am obsessed with a woman I know nothing about, but at the same time I feel as if I have known her in a different life. I don't believe in that shit. When you die, you die, but since feeling her, feeling the pain slowly fade, I am trying to think logically. I am trying to figure out why I am becoming this way with her. But maybe there is just no logic, no reasoning. She is my reason, my ice. My cure that I have been searching for.

Now I just have to find her again, and show her, let her see that getting lost with me is something that I can always give her. She melted against me with my words. I can tell she is running from something, but I want to be the one she runs to.

A friend.

A lover.

An escape.

Whatever she needs, I will be there for her. I want more. I want to love her, to break her, and put her back together again, only with me intertwined with her.

Damn.

Stranger danger again! Stalker behavior Cole, bad boy, down, down.

I chuckle at myself and shake my head as I sit up and look at the empty rink. The lights turn off, leaving me alone with the ice.

I take a deep breath as I stand and slowly remove the rest of my gear, leaving me in my undershirt, pants, and skates. I reach down, grab my phone, and quickly swipe across the screen and click on my Spotify playlist. I put it into my back pocket and make my way back onto the ice.

I close my eyes and spread out my arms as I move across the ice, letting the music take me away. I move my hands and legs to the beat of the music. It has been a long time since I just let loose and danced on the ice.

I don't know how much time has passed since I came back out on the ice, but my heart is racing, and my face is covered in sweat. I lower my arms and open my eyes.

Kolby is leaning against the entrance to the ice. His eyes locked on me as I slowly skate over to him, stopping in front of him.

"Watching you dance is beautiful, bro," he says softly.

"Thanks."

"I forget that," he stops mid sentence.

"What?" I ask as I tilt my head, looking at him.

"How beautiful the ice can be without the pain," he says, crossing his arms over his chest.

His words cut me, but they are true. On the ice, when we play, it is all about the pain and pressure to be ruthless and cold, violent even. But when I dance, it is the movements that heal my soul.

I nod, not knowing what to say back.

"Let's go to the club," he says with a smile. He wants to go back and see the bartender, and I want to see if my cure is there.

"Okay," I say, nodding as I walk past him.

Maybe tonight will be the night that I actually see her, and I will be able to validate that she isn't someone I just made up inside my head.

Chapter 14
Brad

Ikeep my hand on her lower back as we make our way through the crowd of strangers to the bar. She's there, leaning against the counter, patiently waiting for her best friend.

A normal guy wouldn't care that the woman they are interested in has a best friend, but I am not a normal guy. It pisses me off that when I came over this morning; it wasn't her that came back to the door to greet me, but her best friend telling me she wasn't coming out, and that they had a bestie day.

What in the flying fuck is a bestie day? I wanted to ask, but I didn't because the anger overtook me. At the last minute, I swallowed it down, the same way I will force Alexa to swallow my cum for not seeing me.

I should come first, correction I will fucking come first. I should have been with her when she got her hair done. What if they used the wrong shade of blonde? What if I wanted her hair cut a certain way? It was my idea. I should be the one that is in control of it.

But I thought ahead and to the hair salon and gave the lady a big ass fucking tip to do exactly what I wanted, and then I waited out in the parking lot and watched her get it done. Then I had to see where she was going next on fucking bestie day. So I followed them for hours, from one bookstore to two other bookstores; who knew there were that many fucking bookstores? Then they went and had coffee, went to a movie, and then topped it off with dinner.

I spent the whole day sending her multiple texts, and her only replying every so often, driving me fucking nuts. But I am not in complete control yet, but I will be soon. It starts with her hair, but it won't be long and I will have her wrapped up in me and before she knows it, I will own her.

I will fucking make her mine.

We haven't had the talk; I wanted to, and we will, but it hasn't happened yet. So right now, all I can do is make sure that every fucking loser in this place knows that she is mine, even if she doesn't know it yet.

I sit on the bar stool, wrapping my arm around her and rest my hand against her exposed stomach from her crop top. I look up at her hair that is up in a messy bun, but instead of the dark brown hair I saw yesterday, in its place is a very light blonde.

She was such a good fucking girl, listening to me about changing her hair color. I told her it might be a good change for her, but really, it was for my benefit, not hers.

My image is everything and I will not be seen dating a woman that is not fit and blond. I will get her to the fit part soon, but for now, her curves distract from the extra fat on her stomach.

She is gorgeous as a blond, and it pleases me that she listened. I thought she would fight me harder, but I finally broke her down. It took weeks. It shouldn't be like that. When I tell her something, she should just do it without question in order to please me, but I will get her there.

I lean in, resting my lips against her ear. Her ocean scent consuming me, "You're such a good girl for listening to me," I whisper.

I pull back and watch her quickly turn and lock eyes with me. Her eyes rapidly search mine. I see worry, concern, but also lust in her eyes. She is guarded as fuck, but in time, my time, they will come crashing down.

"Bestie," Natalie says, pulling her attention from me.

For fuck's sake. I take a deep breath as she not only turns away from me, but moves away from me to hug her friend over the counter. She sets down a shot glass in front of her, and Alexa pulls back and grabs it. My jaw tightens as I her watch her take the shot.

She turns, kisses my cheek, and then heads out onto the dance floor, moving between people until she stops in the middle. She starts to sway her hips to the music, and lifts her hands up in the air.

"She needs to be able to let go," Natalie says, getting my attention.

I turn and look at her. "She is letting go," I inform her.

"I know. I'm just saying she needs to be able to have control."

"She does," I grit through my teeth.

"Good," she says, nodding at me before she walks away.

The fuck.

She has control over things that don't matter, but everything else that has to do with her will be mine. It is the way it should be; the woman falls in line for her man.

I sit back and cross my arms over my chest as I continue to watch her. A small smile forms on my lips as the song changes and so do her hips.

Fuck, I want to see her pussy around my cock, hearing her scream my name.

Fuck me.

I keep my eyes on her as she continues to dance. From the corner of my eye, I see a crowd of people swarm two men as they enter through the front door of the club. Women are going crazy, and I can tell that there are cameras going off outside of the doors.

What the fuck?

I keep my eyes on them as they make their way through the crowd. One of them stops dead in their tracks, and the other continues through the crowd, stopping a few bar stools away from me. He leans over the counter, trying to get the attention of the bartender.

My gaze goes back to the man that is standing still on the dance floor. His hands are at his sides. I follow his gaze.

No. Fuck, no.

His eyes are dead locked on my girl. My heart races as she continues to dance. The man makes his way over to her, and I stand from the stool, but don't move. I wait to see what she will do when she gets attention from a man who isn't me.

The song switches, and he grabs onto her hips, pulling her back against his chest. My chest tightens as she continues to sway her hips. He leans down and whispers something, something that causes her to stop dancing. She quickly turns around in his arms and looks at him. He tilts his face and looks at her. From this view, I can see she smiles at him, then wraps her left arm around his neck, and rests her right hand against his chest as she starts to dance, and he moves with her.

Both of them getting lost in each other.

I make my way through the crowd, keeping my eyes on the motherfucker the entire time. I can see his lips are moving, then he leans down and kisses her forehead. Her body stiffens, but only for a moment.

I stop in front of them. His eyes lock with mine, and his smile fades as I wrap my arm around her and pull her against me.

"She's taken, pal," I say through gritted teeth.

He takes a step forward, but I move her out of my way as I step closer to him. She pushes her way between us and places a hand on my chest.

"Guys, stop."

"She is mine, friend," I snap.

"Wait, I am no ones," she snaps back, getting my attention. My jaw tightens as I keep my eyes on him. His eyes are no longer on me, but on her. His expression softens as he stands still.

"Okay," he says as the song changes.

"Brad, go. I will be right there, okay?"

"What the fuck, Alexa?"

"Please."

"You heard her, Brad."

I go to take a step forward, but now both of her hands are on my chest, pushing me. I take a step back, then turn around and walk away towards the bar. Everyone is looking at me, but I don't fucking care.

She is mine, and tonight I will fucking remind her of that fact.

One way or another.

It's 2 a.m. I am annoyed and trying to be understanding, but what I saw was one thing; her telling me to walk away was something else entirely.

I didn't fucking like it.

I pull into her driveway and turn off my car. She puts her hand on the handle, and the rage and possessiveness comes over me in waves. I turn and lean over tightly, grabbing onto her throat, pulling her into me.

"Brad," she whispers, making my cock hard and push against my jeans.

"What was that?" I ask barely able to control my anger.

"I'm sorry," she says, but I can tell she isn't saying sorry for what I want her to be sorry for.

"I want you," I confess to her.

"I don't do relationships," she replies.

"For me, you will," I say through gritted teeth. I take her earlobe into my mouth and suck. She pushes up, a moan leaving her lips.

There you go, sweetheart, melt like fucking butter in my hands.

"Give into me, Alexa."

"I can't," she moans.

I run my hand up her leggings, cupping her pussy for a moment before sliding my hands up and into the waistband of her leggings and underwear. She lets out another moan as I push my fingers between her wet folds.

"You will come for me, and you will be mine, understood sweetheart," I growl.

"Brad," she whispers as I tighten my grip on her throat. She opens her legs for me as I insert two fingers.

"Fuck, you are soaked. You like being dominated, don't you?"

"Hmmmm," is the only thing she can say as I work her clit with my thumb. I curl two fingers into her pussy, and she starts to rock and push against my hand, needing more friction. I turn her head, smashing my lips to hers. She opens her mouth to moan but I shove my tongue into her mouth, taking the moan from her.

"Please," she moans into my mouth.

"Please what?" I say into her mouth, pulling back as I continue to finger fuck her, feeling her juices on my fingers. I can't wait to taste her.

"Be mine, Alexa," I plead with her.

"Brad…" she gasps.

I stop my motion and force her to look at me. She groans, her eyes filled with need and lust.

"Tell. Me. You. Are. Mine," I say softly.

"I'm yours," she moans.

I lean in and gently kiss her lips and start moving again, her body grinding against my hand.

"Good girl," I praise. She moans and screams against me as she gives me what I want. She will learn, I always fucking get what I want.

Chapter 15
Natalie
2nd Month

Isit back on my bed, resting my back against my headboard. I have been trying not to listen to my best friend talking to her boyfriend on the phone. The way he talks to her gives me chills sometimes. He masks it with charm, and smiling, and love bombing her, but I can see it.

He doesn't want her around me, he just hasn't come out and said it yet. He never wants to come out with us, and when she wants to go out, he always gives her reasons he should come along with us.

I am doing the best I can to give him the benefit of the doubt. She is falling for him, and I will do whatever I can to protect her, but I won't force myself between them.

At least not yet.

I can tell he will fight for her, but so will I.

While he is the one shooting the bullets at her, asking her to change for him, without actually saying change for me, I will be right there, willing to jump in front of her taking the bullets.

There is nothing I wouldn't do for my best friend.

I hold my breath as I hear her pace back and forth. She sounds a little annoyed, but is trying to mask it. She isn't the same around him; she is more quiet and reserved.

When he isn't around or she isn't talking to him, she is who she always has been, outgoing, loud, funny, and downright crazy like me.

I miss her; I miss her so much.

My phone buzzes, pulling my attention away from the conversation I can no longer hear. I look down at my phone and quickly reply to Kolby. I can't help but smile as the emoji war has already started this morning.

He makes me laugh, and laugh and cry, and giggle like I am in high school with a crush.

I have never been attracted to a man like I am with him, and he isn't afraid to show and tell me how much he wants me. Kolby not only says what he means, but his actions back up his words, which makes me swoon over him even more.

Bestie and I have joked about how he is like a book boyfriend come to life. It is annoying because it is, in fact, true.

I tried to play hard to get with this man, but damn, he is all the red and green flags wrapped up into one, and I am losing my mind. He makes my entire body light up and come to life.

He came into the bar so much it was driving me crazy, so I gave in and went on a date and so far, the rest is history.

Kolby is hanging out with Cole. They are two peas in a pod, just like me and my bestie.

Cole can't stop talking about Alexa, and I can see it in her eyes, there is something there, something she isn't saying. But I know my bestie well and when she is ready and has processed her thoughts and emotions, she will open up to me.

And I will be here for her in every single way, never judging, only listening and protecting. She deserves to be happy and have a good life and be treated right. She has been through a lot and I will never ever let her get used, abused, or hurt like she has in the past.

My phone buzzes again.

A chuckle leaves me.

"What is so funny, bestie?"

I look up from my phone, and see my best friend leaning against the door frame, man she is gorgeous. I wish she could see it.

"Kolby and Cole want to know if we want to go to the movies?"

She takes in a deep, shaky breath. I can see her wheels turning inside her head. I jump up and make my way to her, grabbing her shoulders and slowly shaking her.

"Please bestie, please," I beg.

"I dont know," she says with a small smile.

"Kolby and I will be a date, but you and Cole are just friends," I say with a bigger smile.

"Right," she says, shaking her head.

"Please," I say dramatically, making her laugh.

"Okay," she nods.

"Yay!" I scream, jumping up and down. I stop for a moment, only to type Colby back.

This is going to be so much fun. She needs to get out, and so do I.

It is okay for her to have fun and have friends, and I am going to remind her that there is nothing wrong with candy, soda, popcorn, and a good movie with two hot guys.

Cole

I have never been nervous about going on a date before, but right now, I am like an anxious little Frenchie. My leg won't stop shaking, my hands are sweaty, and my heart is racing so fast I feel like it might burst.

But I'm fine. Everything is fine.

I jump up from the seat and look down at Kolby and Natalie. They are already sucking face and the movie hasn't even started yet.

A chuckle leaves me, a hand grabs mine, and I turn and lock eyes with Alexa.

"Let's go get some snacks," she says softly and with amusement.

She pulls me forward, forcing me to walk down the steps and out of the theater door. We walk hand in hand back to the snacks.

She releases her grip on my hand. I look down at her; she is resting her hands against her stomach, looking over all the options.

I rest my hand on her lower back, feeling all the anxiety and worry start to melt away. "You can get whatever you want."

"Popcorn and nacho cheese, please," she says as she turns and looks at me with a smile across her beautiful face.

"Nacho cheese? For what?" I ask as we both walk up to the counter.

She turns and chuckles, "To dip the popcorn in silly goose."

My jaw falls open as I turn and look at the kid. His eyes are wide with nerves. I get it, kid, I really do.

"Popcorn, nacho cheese, a diet pepsi, and some skittles please," I ask calmly.

The kid nods and turns, getting our order ready. I look down at Alexa and find her looking over at me as she rests her elbows on the counter glass.

God, she is fucking breathtaking.

"I'm surprised you said yes," I confess to her.

She takes a deep breath, like she is trying to find the right words or something. "It took some convincing."

"Why?" I ask, not wanting to push too much, but needing to know the answer.

"We are friends, nothing more," she says out loud, but I can't tell if she is trying to convince me or her or the both of us. Either way, it is a lie.

Friends don't look at friends the way we do.

She is so gorgeous, but the first thing I noticed was her hair and her clothes. Both of them look different. Blonde has taken the place of the natural dark brown with light highlights, and instead of her typical leggings and crop top, she is wearing fitted ripped jeans and a blouse.

What happened? I mean, she is drop dead gorgeous, but that is not the hair I leaned into and smelled. It is not the dark brown locks I wish I could grab onto.

When I saw her last, she was wearing leggings, high boots, and a fitting crop top showing off her midsection, which is one of my favorite spots on her. She is curvy and beautiful. I just want to fucking lick her, mark her.

But now she is hiding her midsection. Why?

I want to ask her about the changes, but I won't. I don't want her to get mad, and I want to spend time with her.

The questions can wait for now.

The young man hands us our order, and I quickly pay.

By the time we get back into the theater, the movie has already started. We make our way back up to our seats and we take a seat, both of us trying to get comfortable. We both turn and look over at our best friends who are still sucking face.

"Nat, don't forget about air," Alexa teases.

Without disconnecting their lips, Natalie flips off Alexa, Kolby giggles, and I rest my back against the chair, watching Alexa closely, as she sets up her little picnic in her lap.

Popcorn and Nacho cheese, both lying on top of a napkin.

She is fucking adorable.

"What are you staring at?" She asks, looking up from what she is doing.

"You, I am looking at you."

"Pay attention to the movie, Casanova."

A laugh leaves me, causing people behind us to shhh me.

We both chuckle a little more, then turn our attention to look at the movie. I have no idea what the hell is happening, because honestly, the only thing that has my attention is the woman that is carefully dipping popcorn into nacho cheese.

I am so fucked.

Chapter 16
Alexa

Ipull into the same parking spot I have been parking in since I got this job. I turn off my car and sit back in the seat, and look up into the rearview mirror. Once again wearing my hair in a messy bun, like I always do at work, but when I am off, it has been down. I have been allowing it to flow, and I have even spent time curling it.

I am learning pretty quickly what styles Brad likes and doesn't like. He doesn't come out and say it, but the way he acts towards me lets me know if he approves or not.

I take a deep breath and do the best I can to push the negative thoughts into the back of my head, so I can put on a fake smile for my patients and my co-workers. So far, the only ones that know I am actually not okay are my best friend and Cole, the stranger, the man that I have met twice, but can't stop thinking about.

Both times we met each other at the club and both times he used the same line, *"Get lost with me, baby girl"*. Man, the way he said it made me melt. The way the weight in my chest disappeared when he touched me is not something I can explain with words.

He is dangerous; we are dangerous together.

I haven't been back to the club since seeing him the second time. Brad lost his shit and claimed me that night in his car. I said the words he wanted me to say, but now I guess those words ring true. I am his, even though I am having thoughts of Cole.

I am still not used to the new hair, and honestly, I don't know if I even like it. But I will keep it for now. It makes Brad happy for some odd reason. Since the night he made me orgasm from his fingers in his car, and I said I was his, he has made sure to tell me how gorgeous my hair is, and how it fits my personality so much better every time he sees me. But the funny thing is it hasn't changed my personality, or how I view myself, if anything it has made me more critical of myself. But he doesn't seem to care about that. I guess we just have different views on the topic.

I quickly get out of my car and make my way towards the doors. I reach out my hand with my badge, but a hand covers it. I quickly turn and see Cole standing next to me.

"What the-"

He shakes his head and takes a deep breath.

"Cole?"

"Why did you do it?" He asks quietly.

"Do what?"

"Change your hair? Was it for you, or was it for him?"

"Both I guess." I admit.

He tilts his head to the side, takes another deep breath as he grabs my badge and moves his hand, resting it on the device. The lock clicks and the doors slowly opens, and he puts my badge back into my hand and takes a step to the side of me. He rests his hand on the side of my head and leans in kissing my temple and takes a deep breath.

"You are perfect, baby girl. Don't forget that," he whispers as he lowers his hand and walks away. I quickly turn.

"Cole," I yell after him, but he doesn't stop walking, he doesn't turn around, he doesn't respond or anything. I watch him walk out into the parking lot, slowly disappearing into the blackness of night.

My heart races with his words.

What the hell balls was that?

I unlock the door to my house and walk inside to find my best friend dancing with a broom and headphones on. I drop my bags to the floor and shut the door.

She continues to dance and sing, making me giggle.

She turns and looks at me. A smile forms across her lips as she takes off her headphones and pushes something on her phone, connecting the song to the speakers around the house.

Morelly grey comes blasting through the speakers. She starts to dance, setting the broom against the wall. She dances across the room, grabbing my hands and backing up, forcing me to follow her lead.

I laugh as I start to move my hips.

Her smile widens as we both loosen up and dance and laugh together. She always knows when something is wrong, and she knows exactly how to cheer me up without giving too much physical touch. I have issues, mega issues.

But my best friend has always understood me without me needing to say a word.

She will always be my north star.

Chapter 17
Brad

The light from my window comes shining through, making my eyelids light up. A groan leaves me as I roll over onto my back and take a deep breath. I wish I was waking up to her, but I must take baby steps.

I know her pussy will be worth it, that she will be worth it. I just need to wait a little bit longer.

I reach over and grab my phone, clicking on the app that allows me to track Alexa. She is still at her house and has been there for the past nine hours. She is such a good girl.

Slowly, I am breaking her down, and soon she will be completely mine. Soon, I will help activate every thought she has, every action she takes. Every text she sends, every change she makes in her life, every goal she makes for herself will be because I will it.

I groan as a call comes across my screen. I don't want to answer it; I don't want to hear his tone as he tells me what I need to do or what I am doing wrong.

I slide my finger across the screen and sit up in bed.

"Father," I say, trying to hide my nerves.

This man scares the shit out of me, but I respect him. He has made me who I am and has given me the life I have, and for that, I am grateful, but the pressure of being his son and keeping up our image can be hard.

I need control, but with this man, I am nothing and have no control. I do as I am told, just like Alexa will be doing with me. I do what he says without question, just like she will.

I bite down on my lip as I try to keep the groan inside, my cock pulsing just thinking about her doing as she is told.

"Son," my father replies instantly, making my cock go limp and reminding me that she isn't here and I am, in fact, on the phone with my father.

I run my hand over my face. "What's up?"

He chuckles on the other end, but it is not the type of chuckle that makes you smile, more like the chuckle that makes chills go down your spine.

"I need you to run point with the team," he tells me, no amusement in his tone.

I sit up more, feeling my heart race.

"Okay, thank you, father," I say quickly, not wanting him to change his mind.

"Don't thank me, son, just don't fuck this up. Your mother and I have other teams we are focusing on, so you will run point on this one. Understand?" He says in a stern voice, reminding me that this is not a game, and that he can take it away just as quickly as he gave it to me.

"Yes, sir," I say, nodding, even though he can't see me. It is more of me reminding myself not to fuck this up.

"We are flying out to North Carolina this morning, and we won't be back for a few weeks. So please, for the love of God, stay out of trouble and make me proud," he warns.

I can't remember a time when my father was loving or kind. He has never hugged or kissed me or told me he loved me.

Most would say he is a horrible father, but I don't see it that way. He is strong and goes after what he wants. You don't become a famous lawyer by playing nice.

My father has done some shady shit, and I have helped him. We are family, after all, and we take care of our own. No one else matters but our family and us getting further and further in life.

"I will," I say with confidence. I will make fucking sure he doesn't regret this.

"Have you locked down that nurse?" He asks in an amused voice.

My heart stops at his question. Rage surging through me.

"Almost," I say, feeling the need to check my phone to see if she is still where she is supposed to be.

"Make sure it gets done," he warns.

"I will," I whisper, nodding again.

"Don't forget, tonight is one of the private parties; take your girl with you. Let the world see you with her, let everyone see you are settling down. Your image reflects on me," he says in a low, dark tone.

I know how important the fucking image is, which is why I will mold Alexa into what I need and want, what will benefit me. She will see that my way is the best and only way to give her a good life. I doubt she wants to be working as a nurse for the rest of her life; it's way too demanding.

I will need her to go to the parties with me and make appearances. Now that she is mine, what she does and how she acts and who she is friends with will reflect on me just as much as mine does on my father.

"I will not disappoint you, father," I say, trying to convince both of us.

He says nothing, but the call hangs up. I pull my phone from my ear and open the app again to find that she is driving.

Tonight, she will be on my arm, and tonight is the night that she will see just how much my image really matters.

She will be on her best behavior for me, and if she isn't, I will enjoy punishing her.

I pull in front of the hotel and the valet comes to my side and opens my door, while another man opens up Alexa's. I will look past that the fucker took the job that I was supposed to do. Tonight is going to be a good night, our first appearance as a couple, and this will be the moment she finds out exactly who I am.

She hasn't talked much about her past, and I haven't told her who my family is or what I do for a living. I have planned it where she will find out in a situation she can't run from me. So, tonight is perfect. She won't dare embarrass me.

It took some convincing, but I took her shopping, and we stayed far away from joggers, sweatshirts, leggings, and crop tops. I could tell she was uncomfortable, but I don't care; she needs to change because she is with me.

She doesn't need to worry about anything. I will take care of all of it.

I grab tightly onto her hand as our pictures get taken. I wrap my arm tightly around her, trying to shield her just enough that she feels safe, but not to the point where it is hiding who she is.

I need the world to see her on my arm, to see that she, in fact, belongs to me.

We make our way into the hotel, and before we can get completely in, Alexa stops, getting out of my hold. I quickly turn around and walk into her, grabbing her face gently with my hands, forcing her to look at me.

She has the perfect amount of makeup on; the eyeliner making her eyes pop even more than they already do. Her blonde hair is curled and flowing down her front and the rest down her back. The blouse and slacks she is wearing with the heels I picked out makes her entire body pop in all the right places, and the blouse I chose hides the parts of her we need to work on.

She is perfect, or as perfect as I could get her for now.

"What is wrong?" I ask, looking into her eyes.

She still can hide her emotions from me, which I don't like. One day I will be able to read her so fucking well, but right now I am impatient, and I am getting annoyed that we aren't already inside mingling.

"I don't feel comfortable Brad, this isn't me," she confesses, tears building in her eyes.

"You are wrong sweetheart, this is you. You are beautiful."

She takes a step back, making my chest tighten as she motions up and down herself. "This isn't me."

I walk into her again. I keep my hands at my sides, worried about what I will do with them if I don't. "Sweetheart, I promise you, you will get used to this new you, the you that has always been underneath. You just need someone to encourage you and remind you, and that someone is me."

She takes in a deep, shaking breath. If I allow her to stand here for too long, I am afraid she will turn around and bolt, so I do the only thing I can do to ensure that won't happen. I grab her hand.

"We can go shopping tomorrow, and I can help you throw out your old things. You just need to make room for this version of you."

"I like my clothes. I liked my hair."

Fuck me.

"Please trust me, I would never do anything to hurt you. I am trying to help you. You said you don't like what you look like, right?"

"Well, yeah, I struggle."

"So let me help you not struggle."

"Okay," she whispers.

I lean in and kiss her forehead. "That's my good girl."

I pull back and turn, forcing her to follow me as we make our way into the hotel. There are people everywhere, players, friends, family, lawyers, everyone that is anyone for the team is here tonight.

I stop dead in my tracks.

Fuck me.

I look across the room at the bar and see that motherfucker. He is wearing a jersey. Fuck, of course.

He is a mother fucking Dark Knight, and not only that, he is #3, the lead defense man, the golden boy, the spotlight of the team.

Of course he fucking is.

Chapter 18
Cole

Ihate, hate, hate these things. Kolby has always been the spotlight one, the one that holds my hand, reminding me it will be okay. I haven't liked the spotlight since I was a kid, and CPS came in questioning me about my mom.

I didn't like the fact that they couldn't just leave us alone. I could take care of myself, and I could take care of my mom, but the state didn't see it that way. They didn't understand.

I don't blame them now. I know they were just trying to protect me, wanting me to have a better life, and if I had stayed with my mom and she didn't give me up, I don't know where I would be today. Maybe I would have never found dancing or hockey. I am not sure. But the older I get and the more famous I get doesn't change the fact that I don't like cameras, and I don't like parties like this.

The clubs are different. They are dark, and forbidden, and normally, everyone there is trying to escape something and just wants to let go, even if it's for a little bit before we have to go back to real life.

These types of parties are for the players. They are created for the world to see us, and everyone that is spending money, supporting and encouraging the players to come together and see us up close and personal.

There is no escaping this spotlight hell of a hotel.

I take the shot in my hand and put it up to my mouth, I slowly turn needing to scan over the room, before I can put the liquid in my mouth that is supposed to help me deal with this bullshit of a night, my heart stops.

I drop the glass, and the alcohol spills on my arm and chest, but I don't care. At this moment, the only thing I can care about is the woman that is at the entrance of the party, holding hands with that la douche from the club. I scan the woman, looking her up and down. My heart stops when she turns, and our eyes lock.

No fucking way.

That is my ice. Right in front of me.

I watch la douche lead her into the room as people surround him within seconds. She pulls away from his hand and slowly puts space between them and the other people that are taking pictures and asking questions. So many fucking questions.

He doesn't seem to mind the chaos. In fact, he has a fucking big ass smile on his face, like he smoked a bowl before coming into this hotel. No one is that fucking happy to answer questions and get their picture taken unless they are high or drunk, period, but what is chilling is that he doesn't seem to be either. Fucking la douche.

I bring my attention back to Alexa. She has made her way across the room and is now coming up to stand right next to me at the counter. She leans against it while she waits for the bartender to come over.

I lean in, resting my forehead against the side of her head, and take in a deep breath. Ocean, she still smells like the ocean. I am glad that hasn't changed.

"Hey, baby girl," I whisper as I pull back just enough to allow her to turn her head and look at me.

"I'm with Brad," she confesses, as if she was getting ready to say that the entire time she was making her way over here.

"I can see that," I whisper. I saw them walk in together, and I even saw them holding hands, but I also saw how she walked away from him as soon as she could.

"We can't do this," she motions between us.

I take in a deep breath. "I will be whatever you need me to be, baby girl," I confess to her, pain in my voice, as I try to keep my emotions in check.

I would be lying if I said seeing her here with that fucking cock didn't hurt, because it does. It stings like a bee that is trying to protect its home.

"What does that mean?" She asks in a curious but distant voice.

I close my eyes for a moment, trying to calm down my racing heartbeat as the music starts to play. I open my eyes and smile.

"Get lost with me," I plead with her.

"What?" She tilts her head and smiles.

I reach out my hand to her, hoping and praying she takes it.

She does without question. I turn and lead us both onto the made-up dance floor. I can give two shit dogs if we are allowed to dance or not, because right now the only thing that matters is her.

I wrap my arms around her midsection as she wraps her hands around my neck, resting her head against my chest, making me ache. Ache because I want to take away whatever negative thoughts she has inside her head that are telling her she is not perfect.

She starts to sway to the music. I lean down, resting my chin on the top of her head. Her warmth is surrounding me.

I see her boyfriend or whatever the hell he is looking directly at me, his arms crossed over his chest. I give him a smile; I am not afraid of that fuck bat.

"Why did you change your hair color?" I ask softly, pulling back with a small groan. She looks up at me, her eyes searching mine.

Fuck, all I see is pain. I want to take it away, fight every fucking demon inside her head.

"Needed a change. Brad thought it might help."

"Help what?" I ask.

"The way I see myself," she confesses, turning to look away from me, but I gently grab her throat and pull her against me as we continue to sway.

"Has it?"

"No, I feel out of place."

"You are beautiful."

She doesn't say anything. I keep my hand on her throat, refusing to let her look away from me.

"Why did you change your clothes?" I continue to ask the questions that have been flooding my thoughts.

"Brad thought it was time for a change. He said maybe different clothes would help with my confidence," she whispers.

"Has it, baby girl?"

"No, if anything, I feel worse, but I am trying to trust him."

"Trust is earned, not just given."

"What do you want from me? Everyone wants something. What do you want?" She pleads.

"You."

"Cole."

"A friend, a lover, an escape, someone you can go to, to get lost with. Like I said, baby girl, I will be whatever you need me to be."

"Why?" She asks.

"Because you deserve the world, and I intend to give it to you."

I can see the tears building in her eyes. "I don't cheat."

"I'm not asking that of you. Do you love him?" I ask honestly.

"That's a strong word."

"It is."

"I don't know. I think I could. Why?"

"I intend on being your last."

"Last what?"

"Everything"

The song stops, and I can see Brad making his way over. Everything in me is screaming at me to block him from her, but I will respect her wishes. I kiss her forehead and let her go.

He stops behind her, and she turns.

If looks could kill, I'd be dead right now . He reaches out his hand, and she takes it, causing my heart to ache. He looks me up and down and goes to turn around, but I step into him, grabbing his arm.

"I wouldn't do that, Mr. Jackson," he says with amusement. He turns and looks at me.

"Who are you?"

"I am the new lawyer."

Fuck me. "If you hurt her in any way, shape, or form, I will teach you why I have the nickname of 'The Enforcer' on the ice."

"I'm not scared of you."

"You will be, and when I say hurt her, Braddy boy, I mean in any fucking way." I promise.

He groans and forces her to walk away. I stand still as she looks over her shoulder at me.

Fuck, I just made a big mistake.

My ice is leaving and with her everything.

Chapter 19
Natalie
3rd Month

Islowly open my eyes as my phone buzzes for the third time. My heart races with the possibility that it is my best friend. She has been acting weird the past few nights, but I know I can be overly sensitive sometimes. I can feel it in my bones, though. Something isn't right, something seems to be off.

I can't take it anymore. I love snuggling with Kolby, but if she needs me, I need to answer. I roll over and wiggle my way out of Kolby's arms. He groans and rolls over onto his back, and I stop for a moment and gently place my hand on his chest. He places his hand on top of mine, and then grabs my wrist and brings my hand to his mouth. He gently kisses my knuckles, making my heart skip a beat.

I grab my phone, and the screen is bright in the room's darkness. My eyes try to adjust, the phone buzzes again, and I quickly click on the three unread text messages from my bestie.

"What the-…" I stop mid-sentence as I reread her words again.

"Babe, what's wrong?" Kolby asks in a concerned, sleepy voice.

I take in a deep breath as my heart races. What the hell is motivating Brad to do these things? What does he get out of it?

"He wants her to quit her job," I confess.

"Who?" Kolby asks as he sits up.

"Brad," I say, choking out his name. It is like acid on my tongue. I am trying to be supportive. There is nothing I wouldn't do for my best friend, and that includes not hurting her.

Brad is after something. What is it? Her? If that is the case, he has her. She is falling for him, so why ask her to quit her job? Why ask her to change even more than what she already has?

"Fuck Brad, I don't like him," Kolby confesses.

"The feeling is mutual, baby, but we have to try for Alexa," I tell us both. Reminding us both.

I quickly get off of the bed and reach down, grabbing my sweats and crop top, quickly putting them on. Before Kolby can process what is happening, I am leaning over to kiss him on the forehead, and I walk out his front door.

"Bye, babe," Kolby yells from his room.

He knows how important Alexa is to me. Even when she doesn't say she needs me, I can feel it. She doesn't have to say anything. She and I are bonded, and right now, I know she is scared, confused, and needs me.

Cole

I sit forward in the chair, resting my elbows on my knees as I wait for the nurse, or whoever the hell she is, to go get my mother. I hate waiting and being in the open like this.

The funny thing is, I am not really out in the open, but inside these walls, I feel vulnerable. I feel like everyone is watching me, which I should be used to. Hockey star and all; it just comes with it. But the way I am looked at in here is not like I am famous or a star; no, they look at me with pity.

My phone buzzes in my jeans, and I quickly pull it out and hit silent. An unknown number has been calling me off and on for the past few days. I don't answer unknown numbers, but whoever this number belongs to, they are dead set on me answering it.

I let out a shaky breath as I shake my head. I don't have time for mind games, not between what is happening at practice and my mother. I have my plate full enough.

Alexa is heavy on my mind. The date that was actually not a date at the movies went better than what I thought. I was a nervous idiot, but it seemed she was nervous as well.

Friends, fucking friends.

I take in a deep breath and shake my head again, closing my eyes, trying to get a grasp on myself. I don't think it is possible to do so. My emotions are everywhere, my thoughts are everywhere.

Fuck.

I will be whatever she needs me to be: a friend, a lover, someone she can get lost in. I will be whatever she needs, but fuck, it kills me that there is so much distance between us. Kills me; I just can't kiss her and hold her.

She deserves more than what Brad can give her. She deserves to be happy and treated like a queen.

"Cole, my sweet, sweet boy," I hear my mother say in a joyful voice. I slowly stand up and put my phone back into my pocket. I open my arms just in time for her to walk into me, wrapping her skinny arms tightly around my waist, and I rest my chin on the top of her head.

If I hold her any tighter, I am afraid I am going to break her. She is nothing but skin and bones, making my heart ache.

"Hey Momma," I whisper as I hold her close for a few more seconds.

She squeezes me, and then we both let each other go. My heart races as I look her up and down as she takes a step back and then turns and sits down at the table. I follow her lead and sit down as well.

I rest my hand against my face. I sniffle, trying to hold back my tears. I hate seeing her like this, vulnerable, fragile, like anything could break her, shatter her like ice.

"My boy has met someone?" My mom asks.

A smile forms across my face as I drop my hand and nod. "Yes, mom."

"Good, you deserve to be happy, son," she whispers. She reaches out her hand across the table and I do the same, holding tightly onto my mom's hand.

"You just missed your friend."

"What, friend mom, Kolby?"

She shakes her head. "No, not Kolby. I think his name was Brian, or maybe Braden."

"Brad?" I inquire, leaning forward.

A smile forms across her face, and she smiles and nods. "Yes, Brad."

"Mom."

"It's okay, he said he just wanted to check in and see if I was going to make it to any of your games," she says calmly.

Fuck, fuck, fuck.

I take in a deep, shaky breath.

"Don't worry about my games. I just want you to get better, okay, and no more talking to anyone but me, Kolby, Natalie, or Alexa. Okay mom?"

She nods. "Okay, son."

I slowly stand up, and she does the same. She wastes no time making her way over to me and once again wrapping her arms around me. I hold my fragile mom close, take in a deep breath of her scent.

Brad, fucking Brad.

I don't know what the fuck he is up to, but I plan on finding out.

Chapter 20
Alexa

I look at myself in the mirror, the hair, the clothes. None of it seems like me. It is not me, but I guess I need to get used to the fact that this is the new me. Hair and all.

I run my hands over my face, trying to relieve the stress that is coursing through my body. I wish my body didn't react this way. I wish I felt normal, but that was taken from me. The night my innocence was stolen, it became clear normal was never in the cards for me.

With a sigh, I turn and walk out of my bathroom and head toward my room to grab the letter off of my bed. I look down at the piece of paper in my hand. My heart is racing. I didn't sleep much last night, which isn't new, but this time was because I felt sick to my stomach for what I knew I was going to do today. It took me hours upon hours to write on this stupid piece of paper. I kept erasing what I wrote and rewriting it. I still don't feel it is perfect, but it will have to do for now.

I look over my words for the millionth time, thanking them for everything. Telling them that it is time for me to move on.

But is it, though?

I don't know, but honestly, I just want the conversation to be over between me and Brad. He thinks I should quit and said it would give me time to focus on other things, like reading and my writing.

He seems to reassure me with his words, but it doesn't take away the fear in my chest. My stomach is in knots. He says he will take care of me, all of my bills, my rent, anything that I need. He says he just wants to see me less stressed and said it might help with the way I see myself in the mirror.

He says that a lot. He brings up the way I see myself, and honestly, he isn't wrong, but I still don't enjoy being this naked with him, not in the physical sense, but emotionally.

This will either be the best choice I can make for myself or the worst. The only way to find out is by doing it.

As I place my badge against the little grey box, my heart is beating so fast I can hear it in my ears. I can't believe that after today, I will no longer have access to this back door, the back door that both Brad and Cole have stopped me at.

This is a mess, everything is a mess. I am doing as Brad is suggesting, trusting him. But in the back of my mind, I can't forget Cole's questions.

He wasn't judging, but I could hear and see the concern in his tone and written all over his face. Concern that I am confused about, but I guess if I was a person looking from the outside I might be concerned as well.

I have to trust Brad. He has given me no reason not to, and I promised myself that I would not let my past define me anymore.

I take a deep, shaky breath as the door unlocks and the door slides open. I hold tightly onto the lonely piece of paper in my hand as I make my way into the ER. It is during the day which is odd for me, but HR is only open during daytime hours. I plan on coming back later tonight to say goodbye to everyone.

I clear my throat as I turn and walk down the hallway, turning left into the HR office. The walls are bare, just like all the rest. This room is not welcoming, it is cold, and distant, which I guess is fitting for why people normally come in here.

It's like getting called to the principal's office in high school. You get called, and you get in trouble. I have never gotten into trouble at work; I have never gotten written up or had a talking to, and I feel weird being the one that set up this appointment.

I stop at the desk and take a seat. The woman sitting across from me is sitting back in her chair. She is new, and I do not know how to read her. She clears her throat as she leans forward, reaching out her hand. She is guessing why I am here, and her guess is right.

I give her the piece of paper, and she sits back and looks it over.

"We are sad to see you go, Alexa," she says as she continues to look over my letter. She has been looking it over for a few. I know she has read it. I didn't have much to say or explain.

"Me too," I reply, feeling my stomach tighten into a knot.

"Are you not happy here?" She asks, looking up from my letter.

I shake my head. "I am and was very happy here."

"So, why the sudden change?" She asks in a concerned voice.

"I want to focus on my writing," I confess, which isn't a lie, but I don't think she would be happy to know that it wasn't my idea but my boyfriend's.

Damn, that name still sounds weird, even inside my head.

"If you ever change your mind, you have my personal cell. You are a good nurse, and I would love to see you become a supervisor someday, but I respect your decision."

I nod, feeling the tears creeping into my eyes, but I hold them back. I will not cry in front of this woman. I reach into my pocket and grab my name tag, badge, and the set of keys and set them on the table, pushing them over to her. She takes them and opens her drawer, placing them inside, then closing it.

"I wanted to come back for the night shift and say goodbye. Is that okay?" I ask like I am in high school needing permission.

"Of course," she says with a smile, making some of my anxiety disappear.

"Thank you for everything."

"There will always be a spot open for you here," she says with a smile.

I nod and give her a smile as I stand and turn around, making my way out of the room and back down the hallway.

I don't stop; I don't look at anyone. I just kept my head down and went out of the exit. If I stop, if I say a word to anyone, I will burst into tears.

There is no turning back now.

Chapter 21
Brad

Ilean back in my office chair and look over the five monitors in front of me. I switch back and forth, looking over each one.

She is exactly where she should be, doing laundry, reading, cooking food, and now she seems to be writing something. I click on another screen and a new view comes in. I zoom in so I can look over her shoulder.

Yep, she is writing. Good girl.

She texted me when she turned in her resignation. It took longer than I wanted, but now she has to rely on me for her bills, rent, food, and anything else she wants to do.

She is coming along nicely. Piece by piece, I am chipping away her old self and molding her into what I need and want her to be. She is still on the fence, but as long as she does as she is told, I don't care.

I turn and click on another screen, pulling up all the background checks on the players and whoever else they are associated with. In order to protect the team, and its players, I have to know everything. The media can't use anything if we get ahead of it first.

A few players have pending assault charges from bar fights, but the charges will never stick and will never see a courtroom, not if I have anything to say about it. Luckily, my family's name has deep ties, and my father has many people in his back pocket.

Money can buy anything, including people. Everyone has a price, and if you are willing to do that, you can get away with murder.

I lay out the food on the table, the wine and glasses in the middle, the candles are lit, and all evidence of the other women I have entertained here I have thrown away. She has been such a good girl for me and she deserves a reward, food and my cock.

I hear the front door open and close, and then footsteps down my marble floor. I look up and see Alexa in the white spring dress I bought her with her blonde hair curled and flowing just the way I love it.

Man, she is fucking gorgeous.

I make my way around the table and walk into her. I grab her hips and turn us around, forcing her to back up until her butt hits the table. She grabs tightly onto the table edges, and her eyes go wide as she stares up at me.

I can't control myself anymore with her. I have been a gentleman and have taken it slow with her, but not anymore.

"I missed you," I whisper as I lean down, taking her earlobe into my mouth, gently sucking. A moan leaves her mouth, causing me to growl. I grab onto her legs and lift her, setting her on the edge of the table. I pull back, watching her. Her chest slowly rises and falls, waiting for me.

Fuck.

I grab her throat and pull her into me, smashing my lips to hers, my tongue forcing its way into her mouth. She opens for me, just like the good fucking girl she is.

I pull back, breaking the kiss. I push her onto her back and squeeze her throat for a moment, then I release it and grab her legs. Forcing her feet to rest on the edge of the table, I spread open her legs.

Her breathing increases as I kneel on my knees. I pull up her dress, exposing her naked pussy to me.

"Your such a good fucking girl, not wearing panties for me," I groan as I lean in, kissing down her inner thigh, until my face is directly over her perfect pussy.

I lick between her folds, my cock pulsing against my slacks as I rest my left hand on her stomach and push two fingers of my left hand into her tight pussy. I nibble on her clit, making her knees shake. She grabs my hair as she lifts her hips and grinds against my face.

I push in and out of her pussy, feeling her walls tighten around my fingers, her juices already leaking from her cunt.

Fucckkkk mee.

Her body continues to rock as I eat her, enjoy her, claim her with both my tongue and my fingers. I can feel she is getting close, too fucking close. I pull back my mouth and remove my fingers and she sinks down to the table, panting, as I unbutton my slacks and pull them down to my ankles with my boxers. I place myself between her legs and I grab my pre cum covered cock and place the tip at her entrance.

"Look at me, sweetheart," I say through gritted teeth. I grab tightly onto her throat as our eyes connect.

"You are mine Alexa, all fucking mine." I growl as I push myself into her, causing her to scream out as my cock stretches her tight pussy, which I am surprised and at the same time grateful for.

Her eyes start to fall shut. I slam in and out of her, losing control.

"Say it," I demand.

"I'm yours," she screams out.

"Good fucking girl."

My pace picks up as her pussy wraps tightly around my cock, squeezing me to where I know I won't last long.

Next thing on the agenda, make sure she isn't taking any fucking birth control. I can't tie her down in every way if a chemical pill is stopping my swimmers from making it.

I pull out to the tip, feeling my legs shake as I ram one last time into her, both of us screaming out our releases. I spill deep inside her.

All fucking mine.

Chapter 22
Cole

The locker room is going crazy right now. All the guys are getting pumped up for the game. Each game will prepare us for the Stanley Cup Finals. We will soon qualify for the playoffs and then it will be the battle to the death between us and another team. We will both be known as champions for making it to the finals, but the only thing that matters is who wins.

Tonight, we are playing against the Pythons. They are known for their strong defense team. They will need to be strong to handle me and Wright. He and I have the nicknames as the Enforcers, which is fitting, as both of us get into fights. We are sent to the time-out box at least four times throughout any game.

Normally, I need to keep my anger under control, but hockey is the only time I can let go of my aggression, that and when I lift weights. We all have anger issues; just some of us are better at keeping it under control than others.

Kolby is one of those who can keep his temper in check. Unless someone touches someone that is his or messes with his family, then all bets are off.

A standard game like tonight is three periods that last twenty minutes each, with an intermission between each period for around fifteen minutes. I have never understood why, but I guess some need to calm down. I need to stay in the zone and pumped, and I know the rest of my team would agree as well.

I can hear the theme song start to play and we all stand from the benches and turn slowly, getting into formation as we make our way to the exit towards the tunnel that leads us out on the ice.

I was made for the ice; I was made to leave my blood and tears, aggression and madness on the ice. The ice was made for me; it is one of the few things that can handle me, that understands me, that doesn't judge me for who I am. It takes what I give it without complaint.

We all stand still as the announcer names off each of us, and the crowd goes wild with each player that goes out on the ice. Kolby grabs my shoulder, giving it a squeeze as my name is called, and I skate out with my stick firmly against my chest. As I make my rounds, I look at the seats of fans, each of them wearing our numbers.

I stop dead on the ice, my heart stopping. I try to take a deep breath, but I can't. I fucking can't. In the VIP section is the lawyer and my ice. She is wearing her hair up in a messy bun, with her large black glasses. She is holding a beer in her left hand, her right hand on his thigh, and she is wearing our team sweatshirt with no number on it.

Fuck, how I wish it was my number on that sweatshirt.

She is scanning the ice as the other players continue to show off and skate around the rink. Her eyes stop on me. She slowly raises her cup to her lips but doesn't take a drink.

I see pain in her eyes, and longing.

Fuck me.

A few guys pat me on the shoulders, grabbing my attention from her. The music stops, and we skate to our positions.

Head in the game, Cole.

Stay focused.

I turn my head slightly seeing that fuck nugget sliding his hand up and down her thigh. She is wearing light ripped jeans with Vans.

Fuck.

"Head in the game, Jackson," Coach yells.

Right.

I got this.

There is one minute left in the third period. I lean forward, the puck in the exact right position with my stick. I can feel the sweat and blood rolling down the side of my face underneath my helmet. I lick across my lips, and the taste of salt and iron fills my taste buds. My entire body is aching.

This game has gotten a little rough, okay a lot rough, but they started it and, of course, we have to dish it back. We don't know how not to.

"Jackson, you got this!" Kolby yells from behind me.

Fuck, thanks buddy, no pressure.

I shake my head, take a deep breath, and look over at Wright. He is ready, waiting.

I look back at the team, all of us waiting.

Fuck.

I go left, but fake it, and go right, hitting the puck straight to Wright. I stand still as he moves, dancing across the ice. I hold my breath as he stops and hits the puck. The crowd goes silent as we all wait.

Three.

Two.

One.

Whoosh is the only sound we can hear.

My knees give out, and I fall to the ice. The crowd jumps up and screams as the buzzer goes off, signaling the end of the game. The final score is 3-2.

Too fucking close for comfort.

I turn and look toward my everything.

She is up, with her hands against the glass. She is looking right at me. She slowly nods and gives me a smile.

And fuck.

I'm done for.

It is 2 a.m. and I know Alexa is just starting her shift. I didn't want to disturb her at the beginning of her shift. That would be rude.

I hold the fresh coffee in my hand as I walk into the ER, making my way to the help desk.

"Can I help you, sir?" The nice nurse asks. I can see the dark circles under her eyes. Poor woman.

"Yes, can I see Alexa, please?" I say with a smile.

"I'm sorry, sir, she doesn't work here anymore," she says with a small smile.

"Since when?"

"I don't know, not that long, but she turned in her letter."

"Thank you."

"You're welcome."

I turn around and walk out of the doors. What the fuck is happening?

I jog my way to my car and unlock it and slide inside. I set the coffee in the holder and put the car in reverse. If she isn't here, I am praying she is at her house.

Luckily, she doesn't live far away, and no, don't ask how I know, you know, I had to stalk her just a little bit. I know, I know.

I am not sorry.

I park a little up from her house. I can see her car in the driveway, her best friend's car is gone, and I can see the living room light is on.

Why did she give up her job?

Why?

Why?

What the fuck is happening to her? I can see the changes, but then I see her at the game, and the way she looked at me made me want to fuck her against that glass. Believe me, it is high on the list.

I get out of my car and put my hands in the pockets on my jeans as I make my way down the road and into her driveway, quickly making my way to her front door. I lift my hand, curl it into a fist, and take a deep breath as I knock on the door. My heart races as I hear music and cussing and what sounds like tripping?

A big bang hits the door, making me jump.

"The fuck?" I whisper as the door opens.

Alexa's hair is in a messy bun, little pieces sticking out in every direction. She is wearing a sweatshirt with booty shorts, and I bite my bottom lip so I don't laugh and groan from the sight in front of me. She is holding the vacuum hose in one hand and a ripped bag in the other.

"What happened?" I ask as I look over at her and see the dirt everywhere on the floor. It looks like she had a fight with the vacuum.

"You, you happened," she snaps.

"What?" I ask, tilting my head to the side.

"You knock, I jumped, screamed, ripped the bag that I just took out of the vacuum. Now it's back on the floor where it has made a nice little home," she rambles, taking in a deep breath.

A laugh escapes me. I quickly slam my hand against my mouth, trying to make it stop, but it won't. She rolls her eyes and shakes her head, a chuckle leaves. She is so fucking cute right now.

"Why are you here, Cole?" She asks after a few moments.

My laugh dies off as I stuff my hands back into the pockets of my jeans.

"I went to the hospital," I confess softly.

She takes a deep breath, as if mentioning her job brings her sadness now.

"I dont work there anymore," she says so softly. I can barely hear her.

"Since when?" I ask, looking over her face.

"A few days ago," she replies with little emotion, as if she is trying to dissociate from what she has done.

"Why?"

"Why do you care, Cole?" She whispers, looking at me. I take a step into her, removing my hands from my pockets and grab onto her hips. She drops the bag and the vacuum hose.

"Why did you quit?" I ask again.

"Brad said that it was time for a change and that it could help with my confidence," she says emotionlessly.

I fucking hate this guy. Nothing he is doing is for her benefit, but for his own.

"And?"

"And what?" She asks.

"Does it?"

"Don't do that, stop doing that," she says, pleading with me, but also begging me at the same time, making my cock twitch and my heart skip a beat.

"Doing what?"

"Asking questions in that tone, with that look," she says, scrunching her nose at me.

So fucking cute.

"This is me, and I can't be anyone else," I say with a gentle smile.

"It's not a big deal," she says, shrugging.

"It is if you are doing it for him and not for you. You should always come first, always," I whisper.

I lean in, but she turns her head. I rest my forehead against the side of her head and my lips against her ear.

"I accept you for you, baby girl. Get lost with me." I whisper softly.

"I can't."

"I know," I say sadly.

"Please, you have to go before I do something that I will regret."

I pull back, searching her eyes. There are tears in them, but I know she won't let them fall, not until I leave. I wish she would let me catch her, let me be her safe haven.

"I will do as you wish. I will leave, but I am not going anywhere, Alexa. Do you hear me? If you need me, I will always be here for you, no matter what."

"Why?" She breathes.

"Because you are my ice." I confess.

Her eyes rapidly search mine as the tears finally escape her eyes and roll down her face. I rest my hands gently against her face, wiping her tears with my thumbs.

"You are everything," I profess.

I lean in, kissing her forehead. I slam my eyes shut as a single tear escapes my eyes and rolls down my face. I let her go and turn around, jogging away from her and my reason to be in control.

She can't see it, but Brad is changing her, and I will not let her fucking lose herself to that asshole.

I will protect her, even if it costs me everything.

Chapter 23
Natalie
4th Month

Changes come when you least expect them. Life can throw curve balls. Love can crash into you like a thunderstorm in the sky. That has happened to me.

One moment I am being flirted with at the bar I work at, and the next thing I know, that same man has saved me when I didn't even realize I needed saving.

He has saved me from myself. I never really believed in myself, not like I do now.

Everything has changed since the moment Kolby came into my life, changing everything, changing me. He doesn't realize it, but he makes life worth living again.

I never thought I would find my person. The person who would make me feel whole, feel loved and cherished. The fairy tale relationship that every girl dreams about coming true, that is what we are all after in the end, and some find it and some never do. I was one of those that just accepted that it wasn't in the cards for me.

Then Kolby happened. The man that I never knew I needed has shown me what it is like to be loved, desired, and understood.

I wrap his blanket tighter around my body and make my way onto the balcony. I stare out at the trees. The sunset is breathtaking as the color takes up the sky.

I take in a deep, shaky breath. It seems like more and more things are changing, and even though I am happy, I am nervous and unstable with my emotions and thoughts.

We all have a past that we try to forget, and I have tried to escape mine, and for the most part I have, and I made it out alive because of my best friend. But there are still times I struggle with what I have escaped, and for the life of me, I can't outrun all the trauma from the past, but Kolby is making it easier to handle. He is making me feel safer and safer the more time we spend together.

A set of arms wrap around me, boxing me against the railing. My heart skips a beat for a moment, but then he whispers into my ear, and all the fear and anxiety melts away.

"Hi, Darlin," Kolby whispers softly, making the wetness between my legs increase tenfold.

"You drive me crazy, baby," I whisper back as I let his warmth take me over. His warmth seeping through the blanket. He is like a fucking fire.

"What are you thinking about?" He asks softly into my ear.

"You, always you," I whisper back, feeling my heart skip a beat.

"Mhmmm," he says as he takes my earlobe between his teeth.

Fuck, when he does, that fucking mhm thingy, I melt, melt like ice.

Let me be honest right now. Everything about this man makes me melt like ice.

Cole

I take in a deep, shaking breath as I down another shot of booze. I have lost count of how many I have had, and I don't remember what I am drinking anymore. All I know is that I am losing control.

I have been losing control since I walked away from Alexa, doing as she asked, but I knew in my heart I shouldn't have. She, without knowing it, kept me grounded, and now I feel lost, confused, sad, and pissed off; a deadly combination of emotions.

When she told me her reason for quitting her job, I thought it was bullshit. I think that the way Brad is coming in and getting inside her head is scary and not right. All I want to do is fuck him up, teach him a lesson, and put him in his place.

I pick up the shot glass and lift it to my lips. I close my eyes, allowing a single tear to fall down my face as I down the booze. I feel the burn in my throat as I open my eyes and get off of the chair, pushing myself away from the bar. As I make my way towards the back exit, I can feel someone grabbing onto the back of my shirt.

I push open the door and step into the cold blackness of the night. Whoever has a hold of me, let's go. I turn around, and my heart stops for a moment.

"Alexa," I whisper.

"Who is Alexa?" The woman asks as she steps into me, forcing me to back up and hit my back against the wall.

My heart hurts. "I am spinning," I say softly as I place my hands against the stone wall. My shirt is pulled up, and a soft set of hands runs up and down my stomach.

A groan leaves me, not a turned on groan, more like a don't fucking touch me groan.

"No, I'm good," I say, trying to hide that I am both drunk and annoyed.

"Oh, come on baby, I know who you are, Mister Number Three," she slurs.

Oh fuck, fuck me sideways. My head is pounding and the last thing I want to deal with right now is a fucking puck bunny.

"Lady, I dont want you. I'm spoken for," I say calmly, but I can hear the disgust in my tone.

"Oh, yeah," she says with a smile.

"Yep," I nod, making myself even more sick to my stomach.

"Where is this mystery woman?" She asks, looking around dramatically.

"Not here, but she is real," I confess to her.

"Oh baby, come on. Please let me suck your cock," she says, begging and purring at the same time.

"I am warning you," I tell her, pleading with her to leave me alone.

She shakes her head and steps into me right when my stomach does a big ass turn, and the next thing I know, all the booze and food is now all over her face and down the front of her.

She starts to scream and sob as I place my hand over my mouth. She stumbles backwards and I can see a french fry on the top of her head, making my stomach turn again.

She looks at me and shakes her head. "You are fucking gross," she screams as she turns and runs down the dark street and just her luck it has started to rain.

I slide down the stone wall until my butt hits the cold wet ground and I rest my head on the wall behind my head. I take in a deep breath and try to make the dizzy spinning feeling go away.

Images of Alexa flood into my mind. My heart skips a beat and aches at the same time. I wish she could see what I see when I look at her. She is my reason, my ice. She is, in fact, everything. There is nothing I wouldn't do for her. Would Brad say the same?

No, he wouldn't.

I have been watching her because one I am completely and utterly fucking obsessed with her, and two, I don't trust Brad. He is changing her, molding her into something she is not. I can see it; I can see it so well. It is happening right in front of me, and there is nothing I can do to stop it. So because I can't stop it, I seem to be behind the change by like ten steps.

I take in another deep breath as the rain soaks me, and it washes away the puke and the tears. I allow my thoughts to take me away before I do something I will regret, which seems to be a theme tonight.

Chapter 24
Alexa

Imake my way into the bathroom connected to Brad's room. Sitting between the counter and the shower on the floor is the scale. The little machine that was created from the flames of hell itself.

I don't own one, and there is a reason for that because I become obsessed. My best friend had one, but threw it out when she seen my obsession. She is always making sure I am protected. That girl would die for me, and I would do the same for her without question.

We bring ride or die to a whole new, intense level.

I take in a deep, shaky breath as I stop a few feet away. The mirror is right in front of me as I strip. I haven't weighed myself in a few days, and the anxiety of seeing the number on the scale is putting me over the edge.

It makes me want to run as far away as I can get. But I can't run. I promised Brad that I would do this. He says that he needs to know, and so do I, if I want to make any progress at all. He needs to know what he is working with.

I love food, but I want the body that I have always envisioned inside my head: toned stomach, legs, and arms, and nice perky breasts. Tan skin, perfection, that is what my mother called it.

My mother always said that your body is what a man will remember the most, not your personality. You must be able to please them sexually, or what are you good for at the end? Nothing, she said.

I pull down my sleep shorts and kick them to the side. I stand up straight and pull my crop top over my head and toss it to the side as I stare at myself in the mirror — the mirror that doesn't lie.

I see every single roll, every single flaw. My skin is perfect, almost. At least I have that going for me, but I can see the love handles on my sides. I lift my hands and grab them, pulling them out.

My stomach twists with disgust as I scrunch my nose. I release the love handles and run my hands over my not-so-flat stomach.

I hate the feeling I get when I sit down and my stomach touches my leg, whenever I lean over, of how when I'm resting and I touch my stomach it is the rolls that meet my hand and not muscle.

I hold back the tears as I turn and make my way to the scale, stepping onto it. I can see it calculating, and as soon as the numbers appear, my heart sinks all the way down into my ass.

"Fuck," I snap at myself.

I step off the scale, turn around, and stop when I see Brad leaning against the doorway with his arms folded over his chest.

"What was the number?" He asks calmly.

He is calm, and I am dying inside. My body issues are coming full force to the surface. I want to fucking run, to find a dark place and never come out.

"Not what I want," I reply softly.

He pushes off the doorway and steps into me, grabbing me by the throat. He pulls me against him. I grab his forearms as he leans down, smelling me. His lips stop at my ear.

"What. Was. The. Number. Alexa." He says in a dark voice.

"One forty," I confess as the tears escape my eyes and roll down my face. He pulls back and looks me over, gently kissing my lips before letting me go and looking me up and down.

"You need to eat better and stop taking the easy way. You are dealing with the consequences of your own choices," he says in a harsh voice.

His words cut me, wounding me when I was already bleeding on the floor from the results.

"I know," I sob, unable to hold back my emotions.

"Protein is going to be important. Don't worry, I will make you a meal plan that you will follow. We can fix your mistake," he says calmly and encouragingly.

My mistake. My mistake.

"I'm sorry," I say through my sobs.

"Sweetheart, I will take care of everything. Just do as you are told," he says, as if it is that simple.

I nod. He lets me go and turns around, but before he walks out the door, he stops for a moment.

"We can fix this together," he whispers as he walks out, leaving me alone with the scale, the mirror, and my naked, disgusting body.

Shattering me like ice on the floor.

Chapter 25
Brad

Isit back in my seat at the table, watching Alexa move the salad the cook made her around her plate.

My irritation is already on high from her response in the bathroom. I never ever should have to ask her something twice. But she is still learning, and I will continue to educate her. Eventually, she won't need any guidance. She will do what I want without even needing to think.

Eventually, she won't need to think for herself, because I will do it all for her.

I take a deep breath as she sits back in her seat, continuing to move the salad around.

"Eating the salad will help you, sweetheart," I tell her as calmly as I can.

I hate when someone goes against me; I don't say shit just to say it.

"I'm not hungry," she confesses without looking at me.

I know she is lying. I have learned that when she is being dishonest, she won't look me in the eye, which is why during sex, one of her punishments is her looking at me.

If she disobeys, she doesn't deserve to be comfortable until her behavior is corrected.

"Dont lie to me. You are hungry, you are just craving things you shouldn't be," I snap at her, taking a deep breath.

We are in public. Don't lose your control, Brad, not here and not now.

"It was just salmon."

I lean forward, resting my elbows on the table. Her eyes watch me carefully. As the server comes up to the table, she looks down at Alexa. "Is everything okay with your food?" She asks.

"Yes," I answer for her.

She shakes her head. My rage builds in my chest.

"Can I actually have the salmon and mashed potatoes, please?" She says softly.

"Sure thing," she says with a smile, taking the salad from her.

She walks away, and Alexa crosses her arms over her chest.

"That is not good girl behavior," I whisper.

"I want what I want. A salmon won't change my weight."

"The potatoes will. Have you seen your stomach, you don't need any more fat."

"That isn't nice."

"I am trying to help you. I want to help you become confident when you look in the mirror, but I can't do that if you fight me like this," I confess to her.

She takes a deep breath and nods. "I'm sorry."

"You will be Alexa. Good girls get rewarded, but bad girls, well, they get punished."

Her eyes grow wide as she wiggles in her chair. I love how uncomfortable I make her, both with trying to correct her behaviors and also sexually.

I can see there is a battle going on inside her right now.

She has every reason to be nervous.

If I was her, I would be.

As soon as I close the door behind me, I rush into Alexa, forcing her to drop her things on the ground. I wrap my hand around her throat, forcing her head up as I smell her hair and lick the side of her face.

"Your're a bad fucking girl."

"Brad," she whimpers.

What a sweet fucking sound. I force us both to make our way into the living room. I force her to step into the couch. She falls over it, her ass in the air.

"I told you bad girls get punished," I growl as I unbutton my pants and pull them down along with my boxers releasing my hard cock. I pull up her dress exposing her naked ass. I step up to her and slap her right ass cheek, making her whine and wiggle as I step into her more.

I start to move up and down my cock, spreading the pre-cum down the length of my cock. I look down at her. Her body is shaking and I haven't even done anything yet.

"Are you going to listen to me in public, Alexa?"

"Yes."

"Promise me."

"I promise."

"Fuck, I need you," I whisper as I place the tip of my cock at her entrance. I lean over her body, grabbing a handful of her hair and forcing her head up. I rest my lips against her ear.

"You are mine."

"I am yours," she confirms, making me growl as I push myself into her. She is soaked.

"So fucking wet for me, sweetheart."

"Yes."

"You like your behavior being corrected, you like not having to make choices. Let me make them for you."

"Brad," she moans as her pussy gets tighter and tighter around my cock.

Fuckkkkk.

This was supposed to be a punishment, but my girl has a praise kink and a punishment kink.

Damn didn't see that coming.

I pick up my pace, throwing down her head, forcing her face into the couch. She moans and screams as my cock tears her apart.

I want her tears, and that is exactly what I am going to get.

I always get what I want, and right now, it is her.

Chapter 26
Cole

It has been about a week since the game, since I stopped by Alexa's house. Since leaving her there, I have had this sinking bad feeling.

I don't know why or what is causing it, but I have a feeling that something is not right. And now I have to go to a fucking dinner to entertain.

This is one of the many things I hate about this job, the entertaining part. I sit back in the passenger seat as Kolby drives down the road. His phone has been going off since we got in the car. Alexa's best friend and Kolby have secretly been seeing each other.

I wouldn't say secretly, but he keeps using the word. He has made it clear that he doesn't want the media or others knowing about her until she is ready.

"The only reason I am going is because there is steak involved," I growl, looking out the window, crossing my arms over my chest.

I am like a kid throwing a mini tantrum. I know if I could throw my hands in the air and stomp my feet, I would. No shame, I would fucking do it.

Kolby chuckles. "No, you are going because you make seven figures a year."

"Valid point, and the steak."

He shakes his head as we pull up to the restaurant. He parks in front and we both get out. He hands the keys to a young kid. If I could guess, he is doing this job to get through college; I did the same.

I take a deep breath as Kolby wraps his arm around my neck.

"Let's go in, order, eat, and leave, please," I plead.D"Come on, try to have some fun, okay?"

"This is not fun," I motion dramatically at the open big doors.

He chuckles again and drops his arm; we walk into the restaurant and look around. It is packed, but not too bad. The rest of the team is already here, and I can see the coaches and some puck bunnies sitting on the guys' laps.

Fucking puck bunnies.

Never were into them to begin with. They only want to be seen with us to boost their social media views. I don't like being used.

Maybe it is because of my past, not sure, but letting too many people get close is dangerous, and I don't need anyone using me to get further in their own life. If they want it, they have to work for it. Nothing was handed to any of us players. We work hard every fucking day.

My teammates don't seem to mind. They love the attention. Maybe I am the odd one out.

I scan the room again, looking for anyone that I need to say hi to before sitting down and getting lost in the reason I am here: steak, medium rare, mouth-watering steak.

My heart skips a beat when I see her.

Fukkkkk.

I'm glad Kolby convinced me to come. I mean, the coaches and other people would have been upset if I didn't show up, but hey, I'd rather be in bed watching Netflix. But now there is no other place I would rather be than in this restaurant now.

I slowly make my way towards the direction of Alexa. Nothing else matters, and everything else has disappeared. Even from here I can see she is fucking gorgeous, wearing a white dress, showing off her beautiful skin, her hair is up in a braided bun, showing off her neck, the same neck I want to sink my teeth into, and worship.

I stop at her side; she looks up at me, her eyes light up for a brief moment, her eyes pleading with me, if only I knew what she wanted.

I look down at her plate. The only thing she is moving around is a simple, plain salad.

"Alexa, is that the only thing you are eating?" I ask as I look over at Brad's plate. There is a steak, potatoes, and corn.

I look back down at Alexa. She takes in a deep, shaky breath. "This is the only thing that is on the approved menu Brad created for me," she confesses.

My heart is racing, my vision is turning red.

Did I just fucking hear her right?

No, that couldn't be right.

My eyes rapidly search hers, this mother-

I turn and look at him. His eyes are filled with amusement and pride.

"Maybe you need to be the one who watches what you eat. You nugget fucker," I growl. He stands up quickly from his chair, puffing out his chest like a puffer fish.

The waitress is walking by with a silver tray. I grab it from her hands and before anyone can do anything I swing it holding tightly and then the best fucking thing happens; it connects to Brad's face. The entire restaurant goes silent as his breathing becomes rapid. I step into him as he lifts his hand, resting it against his cheek, and spits out the blood on the floor.

"Next time you want to tell her what is appropriate to eat and what is not, you might want to remember this moment. You are nothing. She is everything. Dont make me punish you," I warn as I pull back.

His head turns to me, blood running out of his nose, his cheek is red and turning purple. His eyes rapidly search mine as a hand on my chest gets my attention. I turn and look down to see Alexa; she shakes her head. Her breathing is easy and stable.

I take a deep breath and nod, taking several steps back, dropping the silver tray to the ground.

I can hear the sirens getting closer.

Fuck.

Back to the clinker again, but the nugget was so worth it.

I hear footsteps coming my way; it has only been an hour. The team can't afford to let me stay in here. The media would eat all of us alive. I am not saying I am sorry to anyone. Brad, the nugget fucker, deserved it.

I would have done worse, but I didn't think it through.

I sit up straight and lean against the wall, crossing my arms over my chest. The man next to me has been snoring since they brought me in. He smells like booze, and his face is all fucked up. He must have gotten into a fight. I would pay money to see the other guy.

I look at the bars and see three officers and Mr. Nugget Fucker standing there.

A chuckle leaves me as they unlock the door and open it. I jump up and quickly make my way to the entrance. The officers walk away, and I stand face to face with Brad.

Half of his face is black and purple.

Fuck, I got him good.

He crosses his arms over his chest.

"If it was up to me, I would let you fucking rot in here, but my father says I can't."

"You always do what daddy tells you?" I ask in an amused voice.

His eyes turn dark, and he steps into me, his face now next to mine. "You seem to have a little obsession with my girlfriend."

"Careful, Brad," I warn.

Another chuckle leaves him.

"I was pissed at first, but now I think this can be fun," he says, taking a step back.

My hands form into fists at my side as my vision begins to turn red.

"What does that mean?" I ask through gritted teeth.

"Every time you talk to her," he says, looking me in the eye.

I take a breath.

"Every time you look at her," he growls, making my heart stop. "Every time you talk shit to me, or you get out of line in any way…"

"What?" I snap as what he has stated runs through my mind, images of my sweet Alexa flood me, causing my heart to ache

"I will punish her. I will fuck her, use her, abuse her. She likes it to a certain point, but you keep pushing me, I will make sure she doesn't. Are we understood?"

"Let me make myself very clear, Brad. You touch her…you hurt her, and I will fucking rip you apart. Do YOU understand?" I say in a low growl.

He chuckles and shakes his head. "She is mine. I own her, and she does as I say," he says in a chilling, dark tone.

Before I can say anything, he turns and walks away, leaving me breathless, shaking and seeing nothing but fucking red.

Chapter 27
Natalie
5th Month

The tears continue to run down my face as I try to control my racing heartbeat. I run my fingers through my best friend's hair, trying to calm her down because she has been crying for the past few hours.

Brad has called her several times, but she hasn't answered, and I don't blame her. She feels guilty for what happened with Cole, and Brad confuses her.

Everything seems to be a mess right now. I wish I had the right words to help my best friend, but honestly, I don't know what to say. I don't know how to help her, so I do the only thing I know how to do, be here for her.

I don't have the best past with relationships. In fact, we both ran for a reason. Both trying to escape the darkness that took us.

My phone buzzes. I look down and see Kolby's name come across the screen. I hit the reject button, and then text him, telling him I will call him back as soon as I can. He was going to pick Cole up from jail after Brad had to bail him out, and from what we all heard, he wasn't happy about that.

Cole

I make my way into the rehab center. My mom is going to be released soon, and when she is, I am going to take her away from this place so she can start over. I can finally give her the life she never had.

My mom was dealt a really bad hand, and now I am in a position where I can finally give her a home. She won't have to worry about money or where her next meal will come from. She doesn't have to give her body for her everyday needs because I will take care of everything.

I make my way up to the check-in desk and write my name down on the paper, just like I have before, but before I can finish doing so, there is a woman's hand on top of mine, stopping me. I turn and look down, meeting the light brown eyes of my mother's therapist.

She looks like she has been crying, and she looks like she is troubled.

Fuck, something isn't right.

"What happened?" I ask, not being able to hide my anxiety or panic.

"She had a little setback," she confesses.

What in the flying fuck does that mean? You can't say those words to an addict's son.

"What do you mean?" I ask, trying not to get too worked up when I don't know anything yet.

"She had a visit from a friend of yours," she says softly.

The fuck.

"What friend?" I ask quickly. I know for a fucking fact Kolby was not down here. He has been with Natalie.

"A man named Brad upset her, and when he left, she tried to get a fix. When that didn't work, she hurt herself," she says sadly.

My heart stops for a moment with her words. Brad, why the fuck is he coming here? And what did he say to upset my mom?

I don't get what his end game is? He wants me to stay away from Alexa. I get that, but why would he go this far?

Something just isn't adding up.

"Can I see her?" I ask in a shaky and quiet voice.

She slowly shakes her head. "I don't think that is a good idea, Cole. I think the best thing is to give her some time."

"Will you please call me when I can see her?" I ask defeated.

"Of course, she didn't use Cole, you hear me?" She says, trying to get my attention.

I nod and allow the tears to escape my eyes and roll down my face. She nods and gives me a small smile as I turn and make my way out the same door I just came in.

I don't know what the fuck is going on, but I do know that something isn't adding up. I know he wants a reaction out of me, but why?

I won't give it to him. I won't fucking do it.

Not this time.

I will not let him win.

Chapter 28
Alexa

Natalie and I make our way into the gym side by side. With our gym bags in hand, we walk towards the women's locker room. She and I have worked out together before, but now I am not here for myself because someone else told me I had to and it gives me anxiety.

Brad told me this morning that eating right won't do anything if you don't work out the right muscles. My heart races as we both set down our bags.

"I really miss you," I whisper to her as I set down my bag.

"I miss you, too," she says, giving me a smile.

I turn and look at the full-length mirror. Tears are already in my eyes, but I refuse to let them fall. I reach down and unzip my bag, grabbing my socks, shoes, shorts, sports bar, and tank top. I throw the clothing and shoes on the bench. My heart is racing. I feel like I am going to pass out as I remove my leggings, shirt, and sweatshirt.

I feel like the air is taken out of the room, and I can't fucking breath. As I look over my body, the only things remaining are my bra and underwear. My eyes scan over myself in the mirror.

"What in the flying fuck is that Alexa?" She asks in a concerned and pissed off tone. I lock eyes with her for a moment. She quickly comes to my side, grabbing my arm, forcing me to turn to her. I close my eyes and allow the tears to escape my eyes and roll down my face.

I open my eyes and look at my best friend. Her free hand is over her mouth, tears running down her face.

"What has he done to you?" She sobs.

I turn and look into the mirror. Shock hits me like a knife to the chest. Brad took a black sharpie and outline my entire body, all the spots that have fat, that I need to focus on and tone. The spot that has the most though is my stomach and sides, outlining the handles I know I have.

"Oh, my God," I whisper, lifting my hands to my mouth. I felt the markings, but the entire time he did it, I kept my eyes shut, and I refused to look at myself as I got dressed.

"Why in the fuck would he mark you like this?" She asks, more anger in her tone than anything else.

"He said I need to make sure I am working out the muscles that need it the most. He didn't want me to forget, so he marked me, so I wouldn't," I confess to her.

Brad is just trying to help me, right? He is trying to be a good boyfriend and point out the spots that need the most work.

I should be grateful for his help.

"Lex, this is not right, this is not okay," she whispers, trying to keep back her sob.

I grab her shoulder and squeeze, trying to reassure her and myself. "He is just trying to help."

"By doing this? This isn't helping anyone," she says, motioning to what he has done in the mirror.

I shake my head and lower my hand; she is right, but I can't disappoint Brad. I already made a bigger deal about the salmon, and look at what happened. I need to stay on track; I gave him my word.

I suck back the sob in my throat and turn around quickly, putting on my workout stuff.

"I am fine, everything is fine," I say to myself and to her.

"I know you, Lex, better than anyone. You are not fine," she says with a sad look on her face.

My best friend has been there for me through everything and I know she is concerned, and so am I, but for the first time, a man is showing me love, and I don't want to not accept his help.

I don't want to disappoint him or make him feel like his thoughts and emotions don't matter.

I see the red flag, but in my mind, it is a red flag I can overlook if it means the result will make me feel better about myself.

Do I like that he marked me with a pen? No.

Do I want to get rid of this disgusting look I have? Yes.

I guess I have to take one for the team.

I look over at myself one last time, and I can see some markings on my arms, but for the most part most of them are now covered.

He has drawn me a map, now it's time I follow it.

Chapter 29
Brad

I walk towards the training part of the facility. If I had it my way, Alexa would have gone to a completely different gym, but with who I am, it is free and unlimited, so why not?

I open the door and make my way into the gym. There are different team members in different parts of the gym, all of them working on a different muscle group.

I have to give it to these guys. They are determined and will spend fucking hours and days in here making sure their bodies are the best for the game days.

I stop for a moment and scan the room, and find Alexa on the treadmill and her best friend is on the one next to her. When Alexa told me this morning that she was going to take her with her, I almost threw a fit and was going to convince her of why she was not a good motivator, but I kept my mouth shut.

I put her through the ringer this morning by marking her body with a Sharpie, which I didn't have to do, but it is my way of punishing her for what happened with Cole. That never should have happened.

He never, ever should be in the picture. He is nothing more than a client that I make sure stays on track. I think I painted him a good picture of what will happen if he doesn't let her go, but he doesn't seem to be that smart.

He won't just walk away, which is why I have other things planned. But first things first, I need to make sure she sticks to the workout, and second, convincing her why moving in with me and leaving her best friend in the dust.

Her friend is going to be a problem. I can already see that, so I will shower her with love and understanding, and I'll tell her how her being more independent will help her self confidence. But it is all a lie, she in fact, will not be more independent. She will and is going to be co-dependent on me.

I take a deep breath as I make my way across the gym, stopping at her side. I rest my hand on her lower back, getting her attention. She removes her ear buds and gives me a small smile. I look over at her friend, and if looks could kill, I would already be six feet underneath dirt.

Lucky for her, she has no control over what I do with Alexa, and she never will.

"How did the workout go, sweetheart?" I ask.

"Sweetheart, you've got to be kidding me," Natalie snaps under her breath.

"Excuse me?" I ask, looking at her.

Alexa stops walking, and so does her best friend, as I make my way between them.

"You heard me," she snaps as she gets off the treadmill.

"Nat, don't," Alexa pleads with her.

"You might want to listen to her."

"Do you have any idea what you are doing to her?" She says, staring me in the eyes.

I nod. "Yes, I am helping her."

"More like breaking her down. Why in the flying hell would you mark her?" She seethes.

I turn and look at Alexa. She doesn't say anything as I turn back and lock eyes with her friend.

"So she didn't forget."

"Forget. How the fuck could she do that?"

"Careful."

She lifts her finger and waves it in my face.

"You aren't fooling anyone, buddy. The hair, the clothes, the job, the food changes and now this. What the fuck is wrong with you?"

"I'm helping her," I answer confidently.

"No, you are making sure she becomes what you want, not what she wants. This is for you and your ego."

"Shut the fuck up Natalie," I snap.

Before she can respond, a man moves her back and steps in front of her.

I know who he is: Kolby, the goalie.

"What?" I ask.

"I don't like the way you are talking to my girl."

A chuckle leaves me. "You need to keep a better leash on your girl," I say as I push him back. His hands form into fists, but Natalie gets in front of him.

"He isn't worth it, baby," she says.

"She right, you aren't worth it, you piece of shit. Get out of here. We don't want you here."

I stand still, then quickly turn to look at Alexa. Tears are going down her face. Cole is standing beside her, half shielding her with his shoulder.

I reach out my hand for her, but she shakes her head.

"You need to choose, Alexa. I am not playing this game. I am trying to help you, and she is getting in the way. So choose her or me. You can't have both, sweetheart," I say through gritted teeth. This is not how

I wanted it to go down, but they are giving me no choice, forcing my hand.

"Get out," Cole says in a dark tone.

"Alexa, you need to choose right now," I snap, my entire body shaking.

"Her," she whispers.

I tilt my head to the side; I heard her, but I can't be hearing her correctly, right?

"What did you just say?" I ask, taking a small step forward.

Cole moves more in front of her, trying to block her from me. It won't work. She is mine. Even now as she is being a bad fucking girl.

"I choose my best friend. I will always choose her," Alexa confesses with confidence, making me sick.

I drop my hand down and shake my head, taking in a deep breath. "You will regret this," I look at Alexa.

I smile and shake my head at Cole.

He has no idea what he has just done, but I am about to show him.

Chapter 30
Cole

Istand still for a moment as I watch the nugget fucker leave. I take in a deep breath, trying to calm myself down.

I look at Alexa, and she has tears running down her face. I quickly turn and take her face into my hands, forcing her to look at me.

"What were they talking about?" I ask, not being able to hide my concern.

"Show him," her best friend says. I turn and look at her. Kolby is standing behind her now, with his arms wrapped around her. She is resting her hands on his arms.

"Show me what?" I ask, looking back at Alexa.

"Promise me you won't do anything stupid," she whispers.

"I can't promise that," I tell her.

"Cole, you guys have a game next week, please."

I stay silent and lower my hands from her face. She nods and grabs my hand, forcing me to turn, and she guides me into the locker room. I can hear Kolby and

Natalie behind me as Alexa releases my hand and turns around. I stop and watch her closely.

My heart is beating so fucking fast.

She takes in a deep breath and grabs the bottom of her tank top and pulls it over her head, and my vision goes instantly red.

I walk into her, gently touching what looks like Sharpie.

"What the fuck?"

"He wanted to make sure I didn't forget what I needed to work on. Look, there are handles, Cole, handles," she says, grabbing her sides and pulling them out.

My heart stops and sinks.

Tears once again fill her eyes.

"You guys need to leave," I whisper in a low, dark tone.

Kolby chuckles, and so does Natalie.

She was brave, standing up for her best friend. Alexa is lucky to have a friend like that, just like how I am lucky to have Kolby.

As soon as I hear the locker room door shut, I grab her throat and force her to back up until her back hits the mirror.

"Are you done with him, baby girl?" I ask, looking into her eyes.

I know the answer, but I need to hear the words out loud, and I know she does, too. She has made it clear that she is not a cheater, and I would never ever put her in a position to make her go against her morals or values.

I know I have stalked her, and pushed the boundaries every single time I have seen her, but I would never cross this line right now if she was still wanting to be with that nugget fucker.

"I need to hear the words, baby girl, please," I beg her as I lean down, resting my forehead against hers. She grabs my forearms and melts against me and the mirror.

"I am done," she confesses, making my heart dance in my chest, and my cock push against my jeans.

Fuck.

I will devour her like she is my last meal, those mouth salivating meals, like when you take out the pizza from the oven, and your entire body shakes with need.

"Everything he has made you feel, I plan on replacing," I whisper as I pull back just enough to look at her. Her eyes rapidly search mine as I tighten my hold on her throat.

"I will show you just how perfect you are, just the way you are. He wanted to change you. I want to love you." I confess with a shaky breath.

I release my hold on her throat and grab the top of her shorts. I slowly kneel in front of her, taking her shorts and thong down with me.

"Tell me you want this, Alexa. Tell me you want me."

"I want you," she says without needing to think.

"You have no idea how long I have wanted to hear those words come out of your mouth" I whisper as I lean in gripping her thighs as I take her clit into my mouth, sucking and nibbling. She moans and grabs my hair, her free hand slaps on the glass above her head.

"Give into me, Alexa," I beg as I insert two fingers into her wet pussy. Her walls grip tightly around my fingers.

A groan leaves me as I taste her, devour her. She tastes so fucking sweet, better than I ever could have imagined.

"Cole," she moans as her hips move, grinding her pussy against me, needing more fiction.

I wanted to take this slow, but I don't think I can. I want her too fucking much. She screams out as her release covers my fingers. I lick and suck, growling into her pussy.

I slowly remove my fingers and as I stand up I lift them to my mouth and open, inserting her release covered fingers into my mouth and suck them clean. Her eyes are deadlocked on me.

I remove my fingers, looking her over, seeing the Sharpie marks he put on her, claiming her, marking her, trying to change her.

My heart races with rage as I force her to turn around. I place my leg between hers, spreading them as far as they can go, with her shorts and underwear still wrapped around her legs. I pull down my sweats and boxers, gripping my pre-cum covered cock.

"Place your hands on the mirror," I demand.

She does it without a word. Her eyes lock with mine in the mirror as I move her to my liking, forcing her to hunch over a little. This position is weird, but I am doing it for a reason.

"Keep your eyes on me, baby girl."

"Why?"

"I want you to watch me make love to you. You are perfect," I confess as I place the tip at her entrance. Lucky for me, we are the perfect ratio for this to work.

I reach around and grab her throat as I push into her wet, pulsing pussy, her release coating my cock. A groan leaves me as I place my hand on top of hers on the mirror and start to move.

"I love you, Alexa. Do you understand me?" I ask.

Tears form in her eyes as I push in and out of her at a steady pace, already pushing myself to the edge.

Fuck, she feels so fucking good.

"I believe you."

My heart beats faster with her confession. I release her throat and grab her hips with both hands. She moans and screams out as she is pushed over the edge once again.

"I am going to cum, baby girl."

"Yes, please," she pleads with me, pushing me off the cliff that is her.

A growl escapes me as I slam into her, filling her completely with my cum.

She rests her left hand on top of mine on her hip and our eyes lock as we both come down from a high I never ever want to end.

"You are mine." I tell her.

"And you are mine," she confirms.

"Damn right I am."

I slowly pull out of her and lean down, grabbing her underwear and shorts and pulling them back up. I do the same with my sweats. She slowly turns around and leans against the mirror.

"Where did you come from?" She asks softly.

"Hell, but you are now my heaven, my ice."

I grab her face and pull her into me, smashing our lips together. She melts against me, trusting me.

I will do whatever I have to do to keep her safe.

Chapter 31
Natalie
6th Month

I make my way into Kolby's house, leaving the door open for him. I can hear his heavy footsteps coming up fast behind me. My heart races as I stop in the hallway. He stops right behind me.

He grabs my throat from behind and pulls me against his body. His lips rest against my ear, as my hands rest on his upper thighs by his hip bones.

My entire body feels like it is on fire.

"Hi, Darlin," he whispers, making me melt even more than I already am, if that is even possible.

Before I can respond, he forces me to walk down the hallway. I grab his arm, trying to keep my balance, as he pushes open his bedroom door and forces us both inside.

He pushes me to into the bed and I fall flat with my face in the blankets. He squeezes my throat for a moment as he sucks on my earlobe. The wetness between my legs increases with each passing second. I can feel his hard cock through his jeans against my back, making me groan and moan at the same time.

"You want my cock, Darlin?" He asks in a low growl.

"Yes, please," I beg into the blanket.

He releases his hold on my throat and quickly gets off of me. He pulls down my underwear and leggings removing them and tossing them to the side, then he spreads my legs as far as they will comfortably go. I can hear him taking off his clothes. He isn't trying to be quiet and I don't want him to be.

He is driving me crazy in the best possible way.

He grabs my throat with his left hand, and with his right, I can feel the tip of his cock at my entrance. He is teasing me, pushing in just the tip, then removing it and moving it up and down my folds.

"Fuck," I moan.

He leans over me continuing to play, as he takes my earlobe back into his mouth but instead of sucking this time he gently bites down, causing a moan to leave my mouth, and right then he pushes his cock into my pulsing wet pussy, my walls stretch for him, forming to his size.

"Oh, my-" I can finish the words. He chuckles as he starts to move in and out of me at a rough but gentle pace. He is both hot and confusing as fuck.

How can someone be so fucking gentle and rough? It is making my legs shake as I grab the blanket, shoving my faces so deep into it I might make myself pass out. I feel him kiss down my back, releasing my throat and grabbing my hips. I push back, needing to feel the friction.

"Fuck, fuck baby," he moans and groans, making my pussy pulse more with his need.

I love it when he says fuck; it is the sexiest thing I have ever heard.

"I love you, Natalie. Yyou are my warmth, the warmth that melted the ice around my heart," he confesses as he slams his hips and causes me to scream out in pleasure.

My entire body tightens as I lose control as the orgasm takes me completely over. Within seconds, I can feel Kolby's sperm filling me up to the rim, his sweat mixing with mine. I can feel it drip on my legs.

Holy living fuck.

He leans down, grabbing my throat, and forcing me to turn my head, his cock still balls deep inside me as I try to catch my breath. My eyes try to focus on him, and when he comes into view, he is smiling, making my heart melt.

"I love you too, baby," I whisper as the tears leave my eyes and roll down my face.

I am completely and utterly in love with this man.

"Forever and always," he whispers.

I smile and nod.

"Forever and always," I whisper back.

"Thank you for being my warmth," he says gently as he kisses my forehead.

He releases my throat and slowly pulls out. My body sinks to the bed, but only for a moment, because before my head has cleared, Kolby has me in his arms, taking me into the bathroom.

God, I love this man.

Cole

My eyes shoot open as I try to catch my breath. My body is covered in sweat. I slowly rub my hand up and down my chest. I lift my hand to look, but it is still too dark to see anything.

Fuck, my heart is racing from my nightmares.

My heart stops as a hand runs up my chest. I rest my hand on top of it, slamming my eyes shut, trying to fucking remind myself that it was all just a dream.

Not a dream, but a horrific nightmare. Alexa is safe, safe here with me right now in my arms. I turn my head and kiss the top of her head as the tears run down my face.

"Cole," she whispers.

"I'm okay, baby girl," I try to reassure her and myself.

She lifts her head from my chest. I can feel her eyes on me, but I can't see her. "You dont have to do that, you know?"

"Do what?" I pretend to not know what she is talking about.

"Act like you are fine when you aren't. We are in this together," she whispers.

"It was just a nightmare," I state, trying to reassure her, but I know she knows I am lying. It wasn't just a nightmare to me, it was what could happen if I didn't protect her the way I should.

She doesn't say anything; instead, she snuggles into me.

"I am safe. I am here with you," she confesses in the darkness.

I hold her tighter against me, knowing she is right. My logical brain knows this, but the fear deep down inside of me is still there, still worried.

I close my eyes again, holding Alexa so close to me that there is no space between us. Her legs wrapped in mine and our fingers intertwined. I kiss her forehead, and allow the darkness to take me away once again, hoping that the nightmares don't take over again.

Chapter 32
Alexa

I grab the towel that is hanging on the hook on the outside of the locker room shower and wrap it tightly around my body. It took forever to get the sharpie off of my body. With each attempt, tears washed away in the water.

I wish the water could actually wash away, not just the marks from the sharpie, but also this sinking feeling. I wish it could wash away all the insecurity I feel deep down inside.

There is a war inside my head, one I feel like I am losing. Some days are better than others. This is why drugs and booze became my way out. They took away these emotions and thoughts. Even if it was only for a short time.

I came here to start over with my best friend, and now I feel like I am nothing more than a burden. I feel like I need to run, run far away, to where the only one that is affected by my thoughts, behaviors, and emotions is me, and me alone.

I take a deep breath as I step out of the shower. My body is sore and raw, but I have never felt more alive than I do right now. I have never felt complete and shattered at the same time. What a confusing feeling this is.

My pussy is sore, but feels so good at the same time. I gave in to my desire for Cole, my passion for him, the intoxicating craving that I have felt since the very beginning, but told myself I couldn't have it, that I couldn't have him. I pushed him away and gave him so many ways out, but the defenseman wants someone he shouldn't. He wants someone who is broken in more ways than one.

I couldn't stop myself. I needed him. I needed to get lost in him. He is my safe place and has been since that first night in the bar no matter how hard I fought against it. It has been six months since our first time meeting, and a lot has happened. And Jesus fuck, I should have given into him a long ass time ago.

His cock is not only big, but it is also pierced in all the right places, and holy cow, I have never felt a full body orgasm the way I did with him. It was intoxicating and dangerous, and I loved every single moment of it.

I am addicted. Just like I was when I first tried drugs and booze. One hit or drink will never be enough, and with him, one will never be enough. I will want more. No, actually, I will need it.

He has officially become my new drug. It's not the sex, which is great, really freaking great. Like that feeling you get when you go into a bookstore and get to pick out your favorite dark romance book; giddy and high sort of good. But it is the get lost in him, completely and utterly lost that I crave now.

He said he loved me, but I didn't say it back.

Do I feel the same about him?

I don't know.

I know I feel safe and secure with him, and I know he has been watching over me for months. The tension between us has been more than intense. It is downright Fourth of July sparks in the air.

I am not ready to say the words, but he didn't seem to mind. I think he is just wanting me to know how he feels.

I make my way into the locker room, stopping by the bench. I turn and look at the mirror, the mirror that caused me tears and the mirror that caused me to scream.

I know why he wanted me to watch us in the mirror. He wanted to prove to me that what Brad said was false, and I believe Cole, I do.

The hand prints from Cole still mark my body, reminding me that about an hour ago, he was ripping me apart and putting me back together again in the best possible way.

I am so screwed.

Everything is so messed up with Brad, and now I have opened the door with Cole. Actually, scratch that, I didn't open it; I tripped and fucking fell head first, slamming it open. But I wouldn't change what happened in this locker room, and I won't change my decision about Brad.

He made the biggest mistake he could have made. He asked me to choose between him and my best friend. That girl has saved me time and time again. She is my everything. My other half and him asking me to choose means he doesn't care about me, he doesn't want me, he only wants the idea of what he was trying to turn me into.

Like a fool, I fell for it. His words, his lies, his charm, and I couldn't see that he was a monster dressed as a prince charming.

Now that I can see him for what he is, there is no unseeing it.

What is done is done, and there is no going back.

I refuse to go back.

Chapter 33
Brad

There are no words to express how I feel right now.

I lost my cool, but I never saw her defying me that way, especially it in front of the entire training gym, her friend, and her obsessed lover.

I bang on my steering wheel as I sit outside her house. My phone buzzes, and the tone goes through my car.

Fuck me.

I click the answer button and sit back in the seat, trying to get myself under control.

"What happened?" My father's tone is annoyed, something I am used to.

"Complications," I answer calmly.

"Jackson is the complication," he states.

"Yes, sir."

"I have only asked you to do a few things in your life, and son, you disappoint me."

"I'm trying," I say trying to keep my anger under control.

"Try fucking harder," he barks at me.

"What do you want me to do?" I ask, since he seems to have all the answers to my life.

"Get her to submit to you. You think you can do that?"

"Yes."

"I have done some digging on Jackson."

"And?"

"He has a mother who just got released from rehab. My sources tell me she is on her way to South Carolina for the game," he tells me.

"I know, father, I have gone and visited her already. She is a nobody."

"There is no such thing as a nobody, son. Use his mother. She is a whore and druggie," he demands.

Fuck.

I clear my throat. "Yes, sir."

"We will be back in time for the game, when I get there, Alexa, better me sitting next to you, happy and in love."

"Yes, sir."

"Don't fucking disappoint me son, you won't like the punishment," he growls as the line goes dead.

I know that a submissive woman is important to my father, but what I can't figure out is why her.

I chose her.

He got on the bandwagon quickly, as if it was his plan all along, which makes no fucking sense. But one thing I have learned about my father is that he is always ten steps ahead of everyone, and the rest of us are just trying to play catch up.

I sit still as Kolby's car pulls into the driveway, and out comes Natalie.

I hate that fucking bitch. This is her fault.

My jaw tightens as Kolby opens the door for her, then jogs back over to his side and slides in, putting the car in reverse and backing up onto the road. Then he takes off towards town.

If I know Alexa's best friend, and I think I do, she will be out all night, which leaves me plenty of time to remind my sweetheart that she is all fucking mine.

I watch the lights go out in her house. I open the car door, get out and walk up the sidewalk to her driveway. Lucky for me, I made an extra key when she was taking a shower at my house. She doesn't pay attention to detail, and it has been easy to make her see only what I want her to see.

I take a deep breath as I take out my keys and unlock the door, stepping inside. The entire house is pitch black, as I quietly shut the door and make my way towards her bedroom.

Walking into her room, I find her on the bed with her laptop in her lap. She stops and turns her head. Her eyes go wide as she closes her laptop and leans over her bed to grab her phone off the charger. I rush into the room and get onto the bed, grabbing her and pinning her under my body. I force her onto her back, wrapping her wrists and pulling them over her head, pinning them to the bed.

"Brad, don't," she begs. I can hear the fear in her voice, the uncertainty.

"All you had to do was listen to me, and you wouldn't," I tell her as calmly as I can in this moment.

"I'm sorry," she says, but I can see the disgust in her eyes. The feeling is fucking mutual.

"You weren't sorry at the gym when you made me look like a fool," I snap.

"Brad, we are done okay, just go," she says, as if it is normal to just dismiss me.

I shake my head and grab her wrists with one hand as I unbutton my pants with the other, pulling them as much as they will go in this position.

"Please stop," she cries.

I slap my hand over her mouth, freeing her hands. She grabs my wrist with both hands, trying to get my hand off of her, but it is no use. I position myself between her legs, pulling up her nightshirt, and finding her naked underneath.

"You're such a good girl," I growl, as I place the head of my cock at her entrance.

I freeze when I see the bruises on her inner thighs.

"Did he touch you?" I ask already knowing the fucking answer.

She whimpers but doesn't respond with words, telling me everything I need to know.

"You are mine, all fucking mine, sweetheart," I growl as I slam into her.

She tries to scream out, but my hand muffles it. I grab her throat. She screams and tries to wiggle away, but I am balls deep inside her. Her pussy is dry, but I don't care, as long as I claim her, remind her who she belongs to. That is all that matters.

"You did this Alexa, you fucking did this," I growl as I continue to push in and out of her.

"You are going to be a good fucking girl, and be with me," I whisper as I remove my hand from her mouth.

"No," she screams, then spits in my face. A groan leaves me.

"I love how you fight, fight for me, sweetheart," I praise.

"You are insane!" She screams.

I still inside her and lean down, our lips almost touching.

"You will do as you're told or I will punish you Alexa, don't fucking push me," I warn.

"Please," she sobs.

"Do as you are told, or I will make you watch as I take your friend," I confess to her.

"No, no, I will do as you say. I will be yours. Please don't hurt her."

"You will be my date tomorrow night to the game, and you will meet my parents and tell them how in love you are with me, understood?" I snap.

"Yes," she sobs.

"Good girl," I growl as I start to move again, losing control. I take what is mine.

What has always been mine.

Chapter 34
Cole

After six months of training and preparing, the game that we have all been waiting for is finally here. Two champion teams are battling it out on the ice and we will leave everything on the ice tonight.

We have all worked hard to get to this point. There is no player working harder than the next. We're all doing what it takes to get not only physically ready for this moment but also mentally.

Imposter syndrome is real, and it is a bitch to get out of. We all have dark places our mind takes us before we go out on the ice. The weeks leading up to this game have us spiraling, trying to find ground, when we felt like our foundation was, in fact, breaking.

After every game we have played, this is the one that we need to win the most.

I take a deep breath as I skate onto the ice. The fans are going wild as soon as they see me. I make my way around the ring as my thoughts are going wild.

I look into the crowd and see Alexa and Natalie sitting in the VIP section. I glide their direction and the fans erupt into cheers, getting even louder if that is even possible.

"Baby girl," I shout, getting her attention.

She turns and looks at me. My heart drops with the marks I see on her throat. I know those don't belong to me. She is wearing brown knee boots, black leggings, and a jersey with my number on it.

She slowly gets up from the seat and makes her way down the five steps, stopping in front of the glass.

"Are you okay?" I ask, resting my hand against the glass.

She shakes her head and raises her hand, resting it against the glass.

"I am going to fucking kill him," I whisper in a low, dark voice.

"Replace him, please," she begs me.

"What?" I ask, but I heard her. I know what she is asking, but I need to hear it again. I need to know it's not just something I made up because it is what I want to hear come from her mouth.

Her eyes lock with mine.

"After you win this game, replace him, please. Heal my wounds," she pleads with me.

"I will, I promise. I got you, baby girl," I say with confidence.

A single tear rolls down her face, and she quickly wipes it away.

I want to ask what he did, but by the look in her eyes and the marks on her skin, I can guess what he took.

We both lower our hands from the glass.

"I love you, Alexa. This win is for you," I confess.

A small smile appears on her mouth. She nods.

"Jackson," Coach yells.

She nods again and motions for me to go. I turn and force myself to skate across the ice, getting into the position that was made for me. I take in a deep breath as the buzzer goes off, and the battle to the death begins.

I continue putting my stuff in the bag. The guys left already to go to the bar to celebrate our win and to let off some steam. I don't think people realize how much it takes out of us to get to this level, to be like this. It doesn't come easily, nothing we have comes easily.

I have worked so hard for this, but right now, the win means nothing. Nothing, because the most important thing to me is waiting out by the ice for me.

I saw her during the game and her eyes were on me the entire time, making me to want to win even more. I needed to win, not just for me, but also for her. I needed to show her why choosing me was the right choice.

I know it sounds crazy, but when I am out on the ice, everything else fades away, and the only thing out there is me and what I need to do. But tonight was different. Her eyes watching me motivated me to push harder than I ever thought was possible.

I took out my aggression over what I think happened to Alexa, of what I think Brad did to her, and took it out on the ice. One thing I love about the ice is that it is forgiving. I can beat the living fuck out of it, and it doesn't leave. It doesn't judge, and it always welcomes me back with open arms.

The ice saved many of us, and now we are living the dream that most want more than anything, that was me, was is the key word.

Now I just want her. It is crazy how one person can come crashing into your life and change everything, become everything.

I grab my bag and make my way out of the locker room, turning off the lights and refusing to look back.

Another season down, and training will begin again in a few weeks. Until then, I plan on doing exactly what I promised Alexa. I will heal her wounds. I will replace that fucker in every single way.

What is left of me is already hers without question. With no doubt in my mind, I became hers after that first dance in the nightclub. Fuck, she made it hard, but for her I was patient.

But now she is mine after she gave herself to me, and I can't be patient anymore. I need to be balls deep in her whenever I can, and I know she craves the same. She needs, desires, and wants the same.

She is going to fucking destroy me in the best way possible.

I make my way through the tunnel and stop when I see Alexa looking out at the ice. She is leaning against the wall in the penalty box. Her breathing is steady as she looks across the ice.

Fuck, she is beautiful.

This woman has taken over every thought, every emotion.

She shakes her head as if she is trying to get rid of a thought or memory, maybe both. I can help her with that. Standing up straight, she exits the box and makes her way partly around the ring and stops at the glass where we touched hands.

My heart races as I look down at my hand. The way she touched her hand against the glass to connect with mine, and even though we couldn't feel each other, the arena was loud with fans screaming, and my pulse was racing from the game that was about to take place, in that moment, she made it all fade away.

I will never forget the pain in her eyes, for I know that type of pain. The chest tightening, the ache that you can't escape from without help, it is all too familiar.

I lower my hand and look up, watching her closely as she lifts her hands and rests them against the glass, and lowers her head. From here, I can tell she is sobbing.

My heart aches as I quickly make my way over to her, stopping behind her. She stiffens only for a moment as I rest my hands on top of hers and lean down, resting my lips against her ear.

I don't like her sobbing because of another man, and I don't enjoy seeing her in pain. I don't like that. I couldn't protect her from whatever he did.

So I am going to do the only thing I can do at this moment to help her. She will get lost in me, and I am going to get lost in her.

"Get lost with me, baby girl," I plead with her.

Sex is probably not the healthy answer, but it is the best way I can communicate what I am feeling for her. It is the only way I know how to heal the wounds Brad has inflicted on her. I will replace what he did to her with me.

I want her to remember me when she touches her skin, when she looks in the mirror.

"Please take it away, it hurts," she sobs.

I don't need to ask what she means. I know, I know her.

"I got you, baby girl," I whisper as I lower my hands, I pull down my sweats and boxers, and grab the top of her leggings, pull them down with her thong.

She spreads her legs without me needing to do it. I reach between her legs as she pushes her butt out for me.

"Such a good fucking girl," I growl as I push in two fingers.

She moans but whimpers, telling me she is sore. I am going to kill that motherfucker. I want to take her away, lock her up in my house, and protect her from everything and everyone.

I remove my fingers, placing my right hand on her lower back, pushing her down a little more. Her ass comes up, making me groan and growl at the same time. I grab my hard cock by the base and place the tip at her entrance.

"I love you, Alexa. I have loved you since the moment I danced with you at the club. I am obsessed with you. I need you."

"I am right here," she whispers as I push into her.

She moans against the glass as I place my hand back on top of hers. I lean down kissing her neck as her ass pushes against me, making me groan, as her walls wrap tightly around me.

"I will replace him, I promise," I say through gritted teeth.

"You already are," she says softly, making my heart ache for a whole new reason.

She is finally letting her guard down with me. I can tell by her tone she is as addicted to this, to us, as I am.

"I promise I am not going anywhere."

"Please don't let me run," she pleads.

"Never, wherever you run to, I will follow, where you go, I will go with you," I promise to her as I lower my hands and grab tightly onto her hips as I continue to push in and out of her. My head falls back and my eyes slam shut as her moans fill the arena and my balls tighten right as her pussy clenches my cock, making it hard to breathe.

"I am going to cum, baby girl."

"Yes, please," she begs, sending me over the edge.

I tightened my grip on her hips as I pull out to the tip and ram back into her, going balls deep. A moan escapes both of us. I rest my hands back over hers, needing to keep the contact.

There is no going back now.

Chapter 35
Alexa

"*Alexa, remember sweetie, stay quiet,*" he whispers into my ear as he places his legs between mine. *He grabs my leg and keeps it resting on his hips as his free hand slides down my front and cups my private part.*

"Please uncle, don't, they will hear you."

He nibbles my earlobe, causing my entire body to shake with chills.

"Everything will be okay Alexa," he confesses, but there is no confidence in his voice, only desire and need.

Both making me want to throw up. I slam my eyes shut as he grabs his dick and places the tip at my private parts entrance.

"Don't act like you didn't miss me, sweetie."

I just want to die right now. I am tired and alone, and right now, he will be ripping me apart once again. I am cut into pieces that will never fit again.

I am nothing but this messed up girl with the perfect parents.

What am I supposed to do? Scream? Cry? Stay silent?

Every single pathway will lead down more heartache and pain. So I do the only thing I know will assure me I won't get hit. I remain silent as the tears soak into my pillow. My bed starts to creak and my heart stops with the act that will change everything.

I open my eyes and my heart pounds out of my chest. The tears slowly roll down my face. I turn my face for a moment, trying to get them off of me.

I forget where I am just for a moment, but quickly the memories of after the game, and me agreeing to come back to Cole's place floods into my mind, causing the anxiety and uncertainty to melt away as if it never existed to begin with.

The nightmare disappears as I try to focus on what is real, and not just inside my head.

My eyes try to adjust to the room but it is dark, pitch black dark, telling me it is still nighttime. I feel a strong arm around me and I tighten my grip on the arm and snuggle in. Normally I wouldn't do this, I wouldn't snuggle. I wouldn't allow myself to be vulnerable, but Cole has broken down my walls.

I take in a deep breath, and his scent consumes me. I can't say how he makes me feel. I can't pinpoint this peaceful feeling inside my chest, because for so long, all I have felt is pain and heaviness. But with Cole, he takes it away, just by being near me.

I am addicted to this feeling.

Addicted to this safety.

I am addicted to him.

He snuggles into me, his lips against my neck.

"I love you, baby girl," he whispers in a sleepy voice.

My heart melts as I hold back the tears in my eyes. He is so sweet, it really freaking hurts sometimes. How can he be like this? How can he be telling the truth?

God, I am in so much trouble.

"I love you too," I confess.

He has said it to me, and I haven't said it back, not because I don't feel it, but because I was afraid. I don't trust people, and after Brad, I feel confused, and used, but in a different way than I have been in the past.

I didn't realize that there are different ways a person can use you, break you. But Brad should get a medal for what he has done. He fooled me.

It is hard to explain, but Brad mind fucked me, and I fell for every word, every action, every smile he gave. I did what he wanted me to do, because he made me believe he could help me heal. But in the end, he hurt me worse than anyone else had before.

I can feel my heart race so fast I can hear it in my ears.

I can hear the groan leave Cole's lips, making my body cover with goosebumps. I know he wanted to hear the words, and I am finally ready to hear them myself.

Cole moves around, making me hold my breath. Before I can react or do anything, he is on top of me, holding my hands above my head.

I am blinking, but I can't see anything. I can feel his breath against my skin, as his tongue moves up and down my neck, then moves to my jaw. A shiver goes through me as his scent takes me over.

Everything about this man is fucking intoxicating and dangerous.

I put the key into the lock and take a deep breath. I look down at my hand holding tightly onto my keys. The keys hit each other, as my breathing becomes more unstable. I know this is the beginning of a panic attack.

I slam my eyes shut as I place my free hand against my chest, trying to make the ache go away, but the memory takes me over.

"Alexa, don't be like that. Spread those legs, like the good little whore you are," he whispers as he grabs my ankles and pulls me down to the bottom of the bed. He spreads my legs as tears escape my eyes. I quickly turn around and crawl away. What a big mistake on my end.

He grabs me by my midsection and places his hand on my lower back, pushing my face down into the pillow. As he pulls my ass into the air I scream into the pillow, but no one can hear me.

"Give into me Alexa, you know you want to. Take it. Take all of me," he whispers as I feel the tip of his dick at my entrance.

I grab tightly onto the sheets of my bed. The sinful, dirty bed that has hidden all our secrets.

Tears escape my eyes and roll down my face as I open my eyes and focus on my shaking hand that is still gripped tightly around my keys. All I need to do is turn the key, twist the doorknob, and slip inside to grab a few things, then slip back out and close the door.

It should be simple and easy, but for the life of me, I can't bring myself to make the moves necessary for this to be over so I can head back over to where I have a feeling I was always meant to be.

I don't want to be here, but I need to get a few of my things. I wish I could just buy everything brand new. I feel like this house and every single thing inside is wrong, out of place, and not mine anymore.

It's hard to explain, but it is just like my skin. It doesn't matter how many showers I take or how much soap I use, I can't get Brad's smell, touch, and breath off my skin. I feel dirty, so freaking dirty.

I think it is the same as my house. No matter what I think of when trying to make it different, the only thing I can see is Brad. His words, his face, his eyes, those dark, remorseless eyes.

Natalie is staying with Kolby, and Cole said I can stay with him.

Brad has destroyed this house for me, has tainted it with a memory I can't escape. Cole is trying to replace the disgusting feeling I feel on my skin, and for a short time, he does.

Cole reminds me he is not Brad, that he is better, that he can replace him. That everything Brad has tried to do, Cole is trying to undo.

I will never forget him claiming me after they won the game, my hands against the glass as I look out at the ice, the ring that seems to make everything melt away.

The man who seems to repeatedly want to prove to me he is real, true, and will never let me go. He is the man that shouldn't want me at all, but he refuses to live without me, and now I refuse to live without him, because before I wasn't really living I was just surviving, I want to do more than just survive. I want to be happy and get lost in someone that wants to get lost in me just as much.

I turn the key and grab the doorknob, a small smile forms across my face as I shake my head, I take a deep breath as I push the door open, but before i can do anything, a cloth is over my mouth and nose, and an arm wraps tightly around my stomach pulling me back.

I feel lips against my ear as my vision blurs.

"I told you, you were mine, sweetheart," he confesses into my ear.

"No," I whisper as everything goes black.

Chapter 36
Cole

Ipull out my phone and swipe across the screen.

Opening the app tab, I find and click on the 360 app and wait for it to load. I love this app, but I hate that I fucking have to use it right now. She should be here with me, eating popcorn, and my tongue deep inside her pulsing wet pussy.

My heart races when I find that Alexa is still at her house and has been there for three hours, three fucking hours. I double-click on her face, and watch as the screen zooms in. I wish you could actually see the person in real time, but you can't; it only shows that her phone is right on the inside of her house.

Worry takes me over, and my anxiety consumes me. I trust her, I do, but I will always need to know where she is and who she is with. She is mine, and I am hers.

I have a bad fucking feeling, a feeling I can't shake. I wasn't at the training gym for that long. She should have been back hours ago and should have beaten me here. She was only going to grab a few things and be back. I should have gone with her, but I had to go to the training gym and do a few things. There is no way I should be here without her. It just doesn't add up.

Fuck.

The sound of the doorbell echoes throughout my house, making me jump and drop my phone. Fuck me.

I pick it up and take a deep breath. So fucking jumpy. I quickly turn around and make my way down the hall, through the living room. I grab the doorknob and twist it, opening the door.

Standing in front of me are Kolby and Natalie. I lower my phone to my side as I look at my girl's best friend, my best friend's girl.

"What?" I ask, looking her over. The look in her eyes is making me sick to my stomach.

"Have you heard from Alexa?" She asks, pulling out her phone and looking down at the 360 app.

I slowly shake my head. "No, you?"

"No, that is the weird part. She always answers me, always," she says with concern and worry in her voice.

"I know," I say back. That is the only thing I can say.

We all stand in silence for a few moments. I feel like the air is getting sucked out of the room.

Kolby clears his throat and steps forward, grabbing my shoulder and squeezing it. "Let's go to her house and see what is going on," he says calmly.

I nod. I don't know what else to do right now. I had a bad feeling before, and now the feeling has only intensified since Alexa's best friend has shown up at my house looking for her.

We both share the 360 app with Alexa, and now I know I am not crazy, and that I am not the only one worried.

The only thing we can do is go to her house and check on her. I have learned my fucking lesson. I will never let her leave my side again.

I pull into her driveway, and Kolby pulls in behind me. He was riding my ass all the entire way here. I swear I was going way over the speed limit, and I don't fucking care. All I care about is getting Alexa and taking her back home to where she belongs. Where I can take care of her and love and protect her.

My heart is aching, my vision is nothing but blurring red., and my mind is racing with all the horrible things that could have happened to her, all of my nightmares coming to the surface.

Fuck.

How could I have been so stupid? I should have gone with her, and now, sitting in her driveway, I am kicking myself in the ass.

I look down at my phone again. Her phone is still inside, and my heart stops when I look up at the door and find that it is cracked opened with her keys still in the lock.

I rush out of my car, leaving the door open as I run to the open door. I can hear Kolby and Natalie behind me, both of them just as worried as I am. Natalie is losing her mind, and I don't blame her. She is the only other person I know of that cares about Alexa as much as I do.

"Baby Girl," I yell as I step onto the porch. Placing my hand on the door, I push it open a little bit more.

I look down at the floor and see her wallet and phone on the ground. Her screen lights up, showing all of my missed calls and text messages, but it's not just my name across the screen; it is Natalie's and Brad's as well.

"Alexa," I yell as I storm the rest of the way in, quickly making it deeper into her house. I open her bedroom door, nothing.

I check her bathroom, turning on the light. Nothing again.

My heart is racing so fast now, I think I might pass out.

What the fuck?

I make my way back down the hallway, stopping once I get into the living room. Natalie is kneeling down, holding her best friend's phone and wallet.

She looks up at me, her breathing is rapid and unsteady, as her eyes rapidly search mine. Kolby kneels beside her, wrapping his arm around her. She falls against him and sobs.

I stand still, not knowing what to do. I feel terrified and beyond pissed off.

"I think I know where he took her," Natalie gasps.

"He?" Kolby asks before I can.

She nods and looks up at me.

I know right away she is thinking the same thing I am. Brad has hurt her, even after she told him she was done.

The night I fucked her against the glass at the arena. Her eyes told me what her words couldn't.

I know he raped her, claimed her. I wanted to ask her so many times to find out if, in fact, the look in her eyes was telling me what I thought, but I was a fucking coward and knew that I would break, that I would shatter.

I take in a deep, shaky breath.

"Brad took her to his parents' cabin. He always talked about going there, but she always said no. She didn't want to be away from me, and she didn't want to be that far away," Natalie explains as tears roll down her face.

She quickly stands and makes her way over to me, dropping her best friend's things on the ground and grabs my shirt, pulling me to her. I let her; I feel broken and confused in this moment.

"He hurt her, Cole," Natalie whispers, her voice breaking with her confession.

"I know," I whisper, taking in a deep breath.

"He will continue to hurt her," she reveals.

I nod, my hands form into fists. "I know."

"Please get my best friend back, please, Cole," she pleads with me.

"I will," I promise her as my knees give out and I fall to the ground, taking Natalie down with me. Both of us lean in, and sobs leave us both.

We know he has done more than just hurt her. He has claimed her in a way that can never be undone.

And I wasn't here to protect her, not then, and not now.

I have failed her, but I will not fail her again.

Even if I have to sacrifice everything I have worked for, sacrifice myself, so she can be free of that monster, I will without question.

There is nothing I won't do for her, for she is my ice.

Chapter 37
Natalie

My entire body is shaking against Kolby's as I continue to tell Cole where to go. I do not know what we will walk into, or what he is doing to her, but I feel like I have failed her.

Cole had the same look in his eyes at the house, and when he fell to his knees, my heart ached.

I should have gone with her to the house. I never should have let her go by herself, but my best friend is independent, and no one saw this coming. But I should have. I am her fucking best friend.

I take in a deep, shaking breath as I look in the mirror. Cole's eyes lock with mine and I look down at my phone.

"Turn left at the end of the road," I say as I continue to look down at the map. Kolby has his arm wrapped tightly around me. He continues to kiss the side of my head, trying to comfort me, but honestly, nothing will until we have my best friend back.

"How far?" Cole asks in a panicked voice.

My heart sinks at what the map says.

"Two hours," I whisper, feeling my stomach tighten into knots.

Luckily, I overheard my bestie when she was talking to Brad about his cabin. He wanted to take her for a while, and each time she had some excuse why she couldn't.

I am glad I pay attention to details, or we would have no idea where to look for her. He made sure she didn't bring her phone, which was smart on his part, but it also scares the shit out of me as to what we are going to find when we finally get there.

I don't know how the hell it got to this, but I will never ever forgive myself if something happens to her.

"Fuck," Cole says, slamming his hands against the steering wheel.

Kolby leans over and grabs his shoulder, squeezing, trying to calm him down, but honestly, nothing will, nothing but rescuing my best friend.

"We will get there," I say out loud, trying to reassure all of us in this car, but honestly, it won't work.

We are all on edge, and emotional, and I have no idea what is going to happen when we get to the cabin, but one thing I know for sure is Brad is going to pay.

Chapter 38
Brad

Icontinue to pace back and forth in the living room, holding the gun against my head as I try to control my breathing. Nothing seems to help me keep control. I hate this; I hate that everything has spiraled into a storm that I can't ride out. I need to escape it, and if I leave it, I am taking Alexa with me.

She was perfect, fucking perfect. I pushed too hard, too soon. I know I fucked up, I will admit that, but it was going to happen, eventually.

I look down at Alexa. She is in the corner; her knees up to her chest, tape over her mouth, and keeping her feet and hands together. Fuck, she is beautiful like this, helpless, vulnerable.

I didn't know what else to do. I was losing her, losing control. I had to get it back.

I stop for a moment and look down at my phone; I have been waiting for hours for my father to call me. He will know what to do.

I have been visiting Cole's mother, and I even pushed her over the edge to hurt herself. Nothing is benefiting me, nothing seems to work.

Fuck.

"Why did you have to make it this way?" I ask, making my way slowly over to Alexa.

I kneel in front of her. She tries to move away, but she is in the corner and there is nowhere for her to go. I lift the gun, and she quickly turns her head, slamming her eyes shut. I watch the tears roll down her cheek as I slowly and gently wipe them away with the barrel of the gun.

A chuckle leaves me as she grunts against the tape.

"You are so fucking gorgeous like this, you know that?" I say in a low, dark voice.

My phone buzzes in my hand. I lower the gun but stay, kneeling down, watching her shake with fear. I swipe across the screen and put the phone against my ear. "Father."

"What did you do?" He asks. His voice is low, but he isn't mad. No, this voice sends chills down my spine. It's void of any emotion.

"What would you have told me to do?" I reply. Alexa opens her eyes and turns her head. For the first time in hours, she locks eyes with me.

"Good boy, so she is there with you," He asks with hope in his voice.

255

I have never fully understood my father's obsession with Alexa, but honestly, I don't blame him. I am obsessed with every single level of my being.

"Yes, father, she is here," I answer quickly.

"Make sure you claim her before they come. You know they are coming," he warns.

"I know."

"Don't worry, I will have you out as soon as possible. Hold tight. This is not how it ends," he says with confidence.

I take in a deep breath, "I trust you, father."

"Good, now get it done, son. I am proud of you," he whispers. Then the phone goes dead.

I lower my phone from my ear, and put it on the ground, along with the gun. Alexa watches me carefully, her eyes growing wide, as I unbutton my pants. She starts to mumble something, but I grab her legs and pull her away from the corner. She tries to scream, but the tape stops her. I rip the tape from her ankles, and grab the top of her leggings, pulling them down with her underwear. She's fighting and trying to turn over, so I let her.

She gets onto her stomach and tries to crawl away, but I am already pulling down my pants and boxers, getting into position on top of her. I grab her hips and lift her just enough to give me the right angle.

Her sobs fill the cabin as I grab my cock and place the tip at her entrance as my legs keep her in place. I lift up on her stomach to keep her hips in the right upward position.

"You made me do this, sweetheart," I growl as I shove my cock into her. Her scream passes through the tape, as I grab tightly onto her hips while I slam into her at a punishing pace. She is trying to use her elbows to crawl away, but it will not work.

She is mine; she is mine in this moment and every moment after this.

"You are mine Alexa, fucking mine," I growl as my balls tighten. This entire situation has me so turned on I won't last long, but it doesn't matter this isn't about lasting, this is about claiming her, marking her, reminding her who the fuck she belongs to, and I know I am getting my point across, each thrust is more rough, taking her fight away.

She stops struggling underneath me. Her forehead is against the hardwood floor. My balls tighten more as I slam into her one last time, releasing inside her, filling her to the fucking rim.

"Such a good fucking girl," I praise her, feeling her body shake even more from my words. She is so fucking gorgeous like this.

I can hear the sounds coming from the cops' cars. I can hear vehicles racing down the gravel road.

"I am not done with you yet, sweetheart, this is just the beginning," I snap as I pull out of her. I lean down and bite down on her shoulder. She screams and struggles, and the taste of blood enters my mouth as the cabin door busts open. I release my bite on her.

"Mother fucker." I hear Cole scream and just like that I am ripped away from her, cock hanging out, pants and boxers down to my ankles.

I turn and look at Cole. His eyes are wide.

"She will never be the same," I snap and spit at him, his eyes go from me to her. And just like that, I see the light leave his eyes. The officers enter the cabin, taking me from Cole, and forcing me to walk towards the busted-down door.

I slightly turn around just as Cole drops to his knees beside her, and I am forced out of the front door.

To jail I go.

Chapter 39
Alexa

It feels like there are hands all over me and it makes me want to scream and move away from them all except for Cole. I want to crawl into Cole's embrace as far as I can. I know one hand is Natalie's, and the other is Cole's. As he holds me close, he wraps me in his jacket before picking me up. I can feel Brad's release between my legs, making me want to throw up.

I don't know who the other hands belong to, but they are emotionless if that is a thing with touching. I shove my face into Cole's neck. His scent and warmth consume me, calming me, as much as it can, anyway.

My heart is racing. I can hear Brad screaming from somewhere. His words hit me like a rock to the chest. He believes what he did was okay, that his kidnapping and raping me was justifiable, because I am his.

How can he believe that?

How can he truly believe that what he has done is justified? I don't understand.

My brain is fuzzy, my eyes are swollen from crying, and my throat hurts from screaming against the tape.

"I got you, baby girl, I got you," Cole whispers into the side of my head as he gets into the ambulance.

The disinfectant sterile smell overcomes my nose, making my stomach turn. As Cole sits down, I tighten my grip on him. I am terrified he will let me go and if he does, I will break. I know I will.

"Sir, we need to look over her," I hear a woman say.

My heart stops.

"No, no, no, no," I mumble into his neck.

"I won't let her go," Cole declares in a stern voice.

"Sir, we need to check her out," the women say in an irritated voice.

If he lets me go, I will scream, cry, and I will freak out, like a kid in a store wanting candy.

"She can get checked out at the hospital. Can't you see she is shaking? I won't put her through anymore," Cole says through gritted teeth. I can feel his heartbeat pounding against my chest.

Cole relaxes a little when whoever wanted to take me from him seems to make some distance.

He rocks us from side to side and starts to hum something. His scent and warmth help me relax against him. I keep my face shoved into the side of his neck, not wanting to move.

I am sore everywhere, and the stickiness between my legs is a constant reminder of what happened to me was real...all of this was real.

Tears run down my face as the old memories of what started me down a path of substance use and sex enter my mind full force, causing my chest to tighten.

"I don't believe you, Alexa, you are lying," my mother says, pacing back and forth with a wineglass in her hand.

I know there are bruises on me. I can feel them. My body aches from what he just did to me. He has been touching me for years, but he never went over the line, not until tonight.

"Mom, he raped me," I sob, trying to get her to hear me, to really look at me, but when her eyes meet mine, there is no compassion, no emotions. Nothing but anger and annoyance.

"He is like your uncle Alexa. You are lying. Why do you keep lying to me?" She screams as she quickly makes the distance between us disappear, and just like that, she slaps me across the face, hard enough that my head turns to the side. Tears sting my eyes as I reach up and cup my face.

Why does everyone keep hurting me?

"You listen here, you little brat. We have worked way too hard to get our publishing company to where it is now. You need to keep your mouth shut, stop telling lies, and do as you are told. Do you understand me?" she snaps at me.

"Okay, mom, I will behave," I say in a low, defeated voice.

I don't know how I should act to make sure I am behaving. I guess keeping my mouth shut about him, about what he does, out of sight, out of mind, I guess.

I slowly turn around, leaving the living room. I make my way out the back door and take off, running down the grass to the enlarged tree. That seems to be my only escape. I am sixteen years old, and should be looking forward to high school, to finding out who I am, and who I want to me.

But now I am afraid this is just the beginning of them, of him, turning me into what they want.

I get woken up and taken away from my memory as I feel hands on me. I am no longer in Cole's arms, causing my anxiety to increase. My eyes shoot open, and I sit up and find nurses and doctors surrounding me, all of them doing something different.

"Cole," I yell.

Everyone in the room stops and then starts again. My heart continues to race, as they talk, and one of the nurses talks to me, asking me something, but I can't make it out through my heart racing in my ear. I feel like I am going to pass out.

I try to get off the bed, but I don't get very far. Hands are on me in a different way this time, keeping me in place.

"No, no, no, Cole. COLE," I scream at the top of my lungs, tears rolling down my face.

I stop moving as soon as I see him run into the room, forcing the nurses and doctors to let me go.

"You can't be here," one of the nurses snaps at him.

"She wants me here. You going to make me leave?" He asks as he moves me up the bed a little. I hold my breath as the nurse nods and motions for him to continue doing whatever he is going to do.

He slips in behind me, resting his back against the frame of the hospital bed. He rests his legs on either side of mine and wraps his arms around my waist, pulling me into him.

"I got you, baby girl," he whispers, and I melt against him.

All of my anxiety, everything finally melting away, leaving only him.

Natalie

I continue to bounce my leg up and down as I tightly hold Alexa's hand, hoping, praying, that she makes it through this. Physically, the doctor said she will recover in a few weeks, but mentally, emotionally, and psychologically, the doctor said he can't help her heal from the trauma, but he said her friends can help, and that I can help her. I plan on doing that. I will be right here. I am not going anywhere.

I let out a soft sob as I quickly wipe the tears away from my cheeks. I look across the bed. Cole is in the other chair, holding her other hand. His head is down as he takes in some deep breaths.

I don't think we will ever forget the screams coming from her as the doctor tried to examine her. Her screams, her cries are forever imprinted inside my mind.

I turn my head when the nurse comes back and I scoot closer, keeping a tight grip on Alexa's hand as she checks her vitals and medication through the drip.

"Is everything okay?" I ask in a whisper, looking at my best friend's face, then I turn and look at the nurse. She gently nods and gives me a small smile. There is pain in her smile and her eyes.

"Physically, she will be just fine, dear," she answers finally. She squeezes my shoulder as she walks by and out of the room.

"Physically," I whisper, looking over at Cole. He is looking right at me, his eyes filled with suffering, pain, and anger.

We both turn and look at Alexa as she sleeps. There may not be any bruises on her face but from her neck down, her body is littered with them.

"I'm sorry I couldn't protect her. This is my fault," Cole confesses, making my heart stop.

I keep my eyes on Alexa, letting out a sob again. "She loves you more than anything, Cole. I have never seen her like this before. She needs you."

"I need her. She can't leave me," he cries. I turn and look at him. There are tears rolling down his face.

"She will never leave you, but you better not leave her. You have to be strong for her, we all do," I say to him, actually saying it to both of us.

A set of hands rests on my shoulders, making my heart race. Kolby leans down and kisses my cheek, then pulls away slightly. "We will all be strong for you, promise," he whispers.

I lean back, resting my head against his chest. He wraps his arms around me, and I grab his arms and hold on to him tightly. Part of me thinks he might disappear.

I need him.

Alexa needs Cole.

We all need each other.

We are a family.

Chapter 40
Brad

The door opens to a cell, and the guard pushes me inside. This town talks so much shit. Everyone in this place knows what happened and what I have done to Alexa. Or I should say they think they know what happened, but no one will understand the bond that she and I have.

She was fucking perfect. She was molding to my will. If it wasn't for that dipshit, Cole, she would be perfectly molded into being my girl right now, but he has destroyed everything. Now I will destroy him.

Alexa is his weakness, but so is his mother. If I can get her to lose control, if I can use her against him, Cole will fucking fall to his knees before me. If my father can make grown ass men cry and fall to their knees before him, then so can I. After all, I am his son. His blood runs through my veins.

I wish I had more time with her, but I did as my father demanded. I claimed her and marked her. I guarantee she is thinking of me right now.

There is no way she will be able to get me out of her head. I will haunt her dreams, and I will stalk her when she is awake. She can never, ever get away from me. Even now we are apart, I am with her.

She will forever feel my hand around her throat, my cock filling her beautiful, tight pussy. She will forever hear my voice in her ear. Cole can try, but he will never be able to undo what I have done to her, and what I will continue to do to her.

These bars hold me now, but not for long, and when I get my hands on her again, I am never letting go.

They are all looking at me, whispering, acting as if they are disgusted, but if they are being honest, I am not the only man who has gone to these lengths to keep a woman in line.

The only difference between me and these fucking pussies is that I actually did it, and they only wish they had the balls I do.

I sit on the edge of the bunk and lean forward, resting my elbows on my knees. I don't know how long I will be in here for, but any amount of time away from her is too fucking long.

I close my eyes and let the sounds fade from the screaming inmates. My entire being focuses on my girl, my property.

She doesn't know it yet, but if I can't have her, no one will have her.

"Stand up, Brad," the guard yells at me.

I hate that they don't care who I am. They have no respect, and it pisses me the fuck off. I roll my eyes, but do as I am told. I have been here for four hours. Four hours too fucking long.

I make my way out of the cell and follow the guard down the long hallway. This place is cold and chilling. They make it to where no one will ever want to come back here.

I hear my father's voice and another voice speaking loudly, more like shouting at one another.

People don't have to wonder where I got my anger from; all they have to do is look at my father, and that will answer every single question they have.

The jail door opens, and the guard steps aside as I make my way out into the waiting room. My father is standing in the middle of the room, pointing his finger in the other man's face.

Darin. I haven't seen him in a long time. He is my father's brother, but he isn't like my father at all. In fact, he scares the living shit out of me.

They both stop and turn, looking at me.

"Son," my father nods and lowers his hand.

Darin locks eyes with me for a moment, then I watch him look me up and down. He and my father look so much alike that it's creepy.

Darin is six years older. He's not successful by any means, does whatever he wants, and has been in and out of prison for many things.

"Father," I say, looking at Darin.

I need to break fucking eye contact. He can see things he shouldn't, like how fucking nervous I am right now.

"You know what you need to do, right?" He asks, looking at me.

I nod and take a deep breath.

"Take her to the lake house," I confirm.

Darin and my father both nod.

"The outcome will not be the same as the cabin, I promise," my father confesses softly.

His tone gets my attention. I have never heard my father so calm and so dangerous at the same time.

"We will be waiting for you," Darin says, making my heart race.

"Why?" I ask, not hiding my irritation.

"Why what?" Darin asks in a low growl.

"Why will you be there? This has nothing to do with you," I ask and demand at the same time.

"Actually, Brad, this has everything to do with me. Her and I have some unfinished business," he asserts.

"Like what?" I ask in a jealous tone.

"It is not your concern, son, just do as you're fucking told," my father snaps at me.

"And don't fuck it up," Darin chimes in.

"I won't," I snap.

Darin smiles and nods.

I don't know what they have planned, but I know what my plans are: make her mine once and for all.

Chapter 41
Alexa

"*All you have to do is give into me, Alexa. It is simple and easy, but you are making it hard,*" Brad says through gritted teeth as he continues to pace back and forth. He has been doing this for the last hour since we got here.

I should have known he was going to try something, but I let my guard down, and now I am here in this cabin, with my ex-boyfriend, who has a gun, and appears to be losing control. This doesn't look good for me at all.

"You just had to make things difficult, and now look at where we are, look at what you made me do, sweetheart," he says softly, which makes chills go down my spine.

"You have no right to call me that," I snap at him, feeling my heart race.

Right now is probably not the best time to get on his bad side, but I am not going to just bend over for him. He tricked me, and changed me, and I won't let him do it again.

He kneels down in front of me and places the barrel of the gun under my chin and uses it to lift my head to look at him. "God, you have a mouth on you, and I fucking love it, I will enjoy breaking that spirit of yours, baby," he says with a smile.

I rip my head back; he chuckles again, then his eyes go black. He lifts the gun and the next thing I know, my head is snapped to the side as a sharp pain runs through the side of my face. Tears sting my eyes as he reaches for something. He grabs my face, forcing me to turn to look at him and before I can blink, his lips are against mine. Then just as suddenly as it started he pulls away and slaps duct tape across my mouth. The tears escape my eyes and roll down my face.

"You are so fucking beautiful when you cry," he whispers.

"No, no, no," I scream, sitting up with tears streaming down my face.

"Baby girl, open your eyes, please." Cole's voice enters my head.

"Alexa," Cole says in a low, panicked voice.

His hands grab my face, his warmth once again consuming me. His thumbs wipe away my tears and I slowly open my eyes. The sun is just starting to rise and as my eyes focus on the only thing that is keeping me grounded and feeling safe at this moment.

"I got you, baby girl," he whispers as he leans in and kisses away my tears, making me cry even harder.

"He can't hurt you," he promises.

"I know," I whisper back. I grab his wrists, keeping him in place, needing to know he is real and not just inside my mind.

I need him; I need him like I need air. I need him to claim me, replace what has happened, but I am terrified and can't bring myself to ask. My body melts into him, his lips rests against my forehead, as I take in some deep breaths.

"I'm sorry," I sob out, barely being able to hear myself.

"You have nothing to be sorry for," he says right back, not leaving any time for me to wonder or get stuck in my head.

I wish I could believe him, I really do, but I just can't. He is in this position, dealing with this drama, Brad, all of it, because of me.

"Do you regret it?" I ask softly, not knowing if I want to know the answer, but it is too late to take it back.

He pulls back just enough to look at me, more light coming through the window, making it easier to see his gorgeous face.

"Regret what?" He asks, tilting his head to the side, his eyes staying on me.

"Being with me?" I ask as tears roll down my face. He gently wipes them away as quickly as they fall.

One of my favorite things about myself is that even after everything I have been through, I have not turned into a monster like those who have hurt me. But in order not to give in to the darkness within myself, the darkness all those people have created, I had to accept that I am broken, and there are pieces of me that are sharp and will never heal.

With that comes insecurities, like right now.

"I want you to listen to me, okay, listen really carefully," he whispers.

I nod and take in a deep breath, waiting to hear the bad news, waiting to hear him say he is done. If I were him, I wouldn't want to deal with me either.

Look at me. I am broken, shattered beyond repair. I'm so tired of trying to hold it together and heal from things I never deserved to go through in the first place. But I can't just sit back and do nothing. Cole has pushed his way into my heart, and it pains me to even think of a life without him. Yes, we have moved fast, and yes, none of this makes logical sense, but love isn't supposed to make logical sense.

"You are my everything, Alexa. You are my reason, my ice. So, no baby girl, I don't and will never regret being with you. I just regret not meeting you sooner," he confesses. I can hear the strong emotions in his voice.

"Please don't go anywhere," I whisper.

"Oh baby, I promise you, I am right here, right fucking here," he pulls me close, letting go of my face. He kisses my forehead and brings me into him, wrapping me safety in his arms.

The one place I feel safe, the one place that makes everything else disappear.

Natalie

Cole gently closes the bedroom door, and even from here, I can hear his deep exhale. He has refused to leave her. We all have. It is taking a toll on all of us. We all feel guilty and ashamed we weren't there for her, that we didn't notice sooner. It took us a few hours before any of us started to worry.

Cole makes his way down the hallway, stopping when he gets into the kitchen. I continue putting the food on the plates. Even though none of us feels like eating, we all need to. We need to keep our strength up, and so does Alexa.

I don't know what Brad's plan was or is, but he is locked up, and Alexa is safe here with us. We haven't heard anything about him since the cops took him away. I will never forget his promise, though.

He said it in front of everyone as they were putting him into the back of the car, that if he can't have her, no one can. I don't think Brad has ever gone this far with anyone before, and for some reason, his obsession is dead set on my best friend.

She has lived through so much, trying her best to stay above water, and still she seems to not be able to escape the demons not only within herself but also the ones on the outside. I can remember when she was at one of her lowest points, she told me I was free, that I could walk away. She said she didn't want me to drown with her, but the truth is I grabbed a floaty and jumped into the deep end with her.

I told her I was never going anywhere, that we are ride or die. That where she goes, I will go. That she will never be alone with her demons, and I meant every single word, and I plan on keeping my word to her, even if it costs me everything in the process.

I finish plating the rest of the food, making sure that each piece of food goes in its rightful place. Kolby is right next to me, washing the dishes. We make a good team. He is something else.

I don't know how to react to him sometimes. He wants in; he has made it clear, but I would be lying if I said I wasn't afraid. What if he runs? What if, when he learns about my past, it makes him never look at me the same?

I don't think he is that type of man, but I am terrified that when he finds out, things will forever be changed because of my past. I haven't told him anything; I haven't opened up about what I have escaped, what Alexa has helped me escape, but I know it will be a conversation we will need to have if I want something serious with him.

We both have confessed our feelings for each other. Over the past six months, Alexa and Cole are not the only ones who gave in to the desire, craving, and pull to each other. Kolby wouldn't let me go, and if I was being honest, I never wanted him to.

I have never had a partner who wants to help, who wants to actually spend time with me, no matter what I am doing; it is refreshing and a little scary.

I turn and look at Cole and find him with his head bowed as he grips the counter tightly.

"Did she fall back asleep?" I ask quietly.

He nods and takes a deep breath. When he lifts his head, I can see the bags underneath his eyes, the lines down his cheeks from tears.

None of us has gotten any sleep since we brought Alexa home a day ago, and when she does sleep, it isn't for that long, because of the nightmares of what happened to her inside that cabin wake her up.

If I could take away all of her pain, I would without question; there is nothing I wouldn't do for my best friend. But right now, I don't know what to do, except just be here for her, listen to her, sit in silence. She seems to be doing a little better, knowing that all three of us are here watching over her.

She doesn't know that the guys have to go to practice. The season is over, but because of who they are and what positions they play, training starts early to make sure they don't lose their edge.

I am nervous; the guys are nervous, but they can't not practice and train.

I take in a deep, shaky breath as Kolby wraps his arms around me, and Cole grabs a plate for Alexa. He turns and leaves the kitchen. I can feel the pain radiating off of him.

It won't always be like this; we just all need time to heal.

Cole

It has taken me years to get where I am, the fame, the money, the status. None of it matters if Alexa is not a part of it. Hockey has been my life; it saved me, or so I thought. I didn't realize I still needed saving until she came into my life. People who grow up in a broken and violent home don't have a cure for what they have been through. We try to escape what we have been through; I found my escape in hockey. Or so I thought.

My number is up, but not for the reasons you may think. Not because of Brad, not because of his threats of what he will do to me, my status, my position on the team, my number is up because of her.

I open the bedroom door and slowly walk inside. She is on her side, taking up my part of the bed. I can see the dried-up tears down her cheeks. She must have cried more after I left, thinking she was asleep. I set the plate of food on the nightstand and take a seat on the edge of the bed. I gently run my knuckles up and down the side of her face.

People who come from the type of home I have, the type of home Kolby, Natalie, and Alexa have, we just want a home, and we want someone who is not going to leave us when we aren't okay.

Natalie hasn't said anything about her past, but Kolby told me that he knows she comes from a rough past. He says he can see it in her eyes, just like I can see it in my girl's eyes.

She has been running and trying to escape, and after what she has been through, I don't blame her, but I want to be the one she runs to, not from.

I don't know how to tell her what I am feeling, so I will do the only thing I can do. I will show her I am not leaving. I will show her that her darkness doesn't scare me. In fact, it makes me want to hang onto her harder, longer, and more intensely.

I lean down and gently kiss her temple. "I will be back soon, baby girl, I promise," I whisper. She doesn't move. Her mind and sleep have taken her from me.

I plan on finding her when I get back. I will follow her anywhere, even if it is to hell.

I hate that I have to leave her, but I can't throw away what I have worked for and neither can Kolby. We can't take care of those we love and care about if we do, and I know that is what Brad wants. He wants us to give up, for us to be so consumed by what he has done that we lose everything.

That nugget fucker will not get what he wants. I will make sure of that. He thinks that she is his, that he has claimed her, that if he can't have her no one can, but what he doesn't realize is that she was never his to begin with.

She was always mine, and I was always hers. I will show Brad that he hasn't taken anything from me, but I have taken every single fucking thing from him.

Chapter 42

Brad

Iroll up and make sure it is far enough down the street; it took some digging and some help from Darin and my father, but the hospital is making Alexa come back for some more tests today. They say I hurt her so badly that they want to make sure that I didn't cause any permanent damage.

I didn't, but they are just taking precautionary measures. I know her and she does what she is told for the most part, but this, her best friend, will not let her miss, and that is what I am banking on, anyway.

For once in her life, Natalie is going to be useful to me and not hurt my cause. I park between some other cars down the street from the hospital. They are keeping watch, but not that fucking closely, and my father told me that Kolby and Cole just arrived at the gym to get checked out by the doctor and to go over their new training schedule.

I knew they wouldn't give up their spots. They thought that was what I wanted, but just like before, Cole was ten steps behind me.

My phone buzzes as I get out of my car. I grab my phone out of my pocket and look down at the text across the screen.

It is from Darin.

Make sure she isn't harmed

He warns.

Even through text, I can hear his tone. He scares the living shit out of me, and even though my stomach is in knots, I nod and quickly text back.

I wouldn't hurt her

I reply, irritation fills me.

Don't believe you. After seeing her face, and her needing to be checked at the hospital, do as you are fucking told.

A groan leaves me as I stuff my phone back into my pocket and make my way towards the entrance of the hospital.

The clouds have rolled in, and from the smell in the air, it is going to be a thunderstorm, one of my favorite things. Storms make you feel as if you are not odd for having unhinged emotions within you.

Luckily, my mother is taking care of the law things for the team, and I don't have to worry about my job for a little while.

Everything finally seems like it is going to go my way. As long as I can get her out of this hospital in one piece and to the lake house, then everything will change for the better. She will finally understand that she and I are meant for one another. She will submit and mold to my will, and everything will go back to normal.

I take a deep breath as I reach behind my back and grab the handle of the pistol in the back of my pants. I keep it covered with my jacket as the automatic doors open and let me in, and then close behind me.

I make my way up to the map and look for the examination rooms. Luckily, I remember the layout from when I met her, before I demanded that she quit. I should have cut her off from everyone and everything. It was my mistake, one I won't be making again.

I make my way down the hallway, stopping at the entrance of the open room that leads to the examine rooms that are separated by curtains. There are other rooms that are smaller, like the one I was in when I first met Alexa. I lean against the doorway, scanning the room and I stop when I see Natalie pacing outside of one of the rooms. The door is shut and she is on the phone.

I am guessing that she is on the phone with Kolby since they should be on a break according to the schedule my father emailed me.

I push off the doorway and slowly make my way across the room. I grip the gun tighter and stop about a foot away from Natalie just as gets off the phone. She stops pacing and looks at me, her eyes go wide. I know she is surprised, but also a little scared.

She has every right to be.

"Is she in there?" I ask softly as my heart continues to race.

She doesn't say a word and doesn't move.

I hate when people don't answer me; I know she fucking heard me.

She finally moves slowly and takes a step to the side, blocking the door. I tilt my head to the side, looking her over.

"I know you heard me Natalie, is Alexa behind that fucking door?" I yell, removing the gun from the back of my jeans. Natalie looks down and begins to sob.

The door opens behind her, and Alexa is standing behind her best friend. She tries to get around her, but Natalie doesn't move.

"What are you doing here?" Alexa asks in a defeated voice.

"You know why I am here, Alexa," I say through gritted teeth as I lift the gun and point it at both her and Natalie

"Please don't do this," she begs, making my cock hard. God, I fucking love it when she begs.

I reach out my hand to her. Natalie shakes her head, but Alexa keeps her eyes on me as she slowly moves around her best friend.

Natalie grabs her arm, shaking her head, "Alexa, don't do this, please, don't do this."

"I can't let him hurt you. Tell Cole." She whispers, and her friend lets her arm go after a few moments.

She makes her way over to me and I grab her, pulling her into me, keeping the gun pointed at Natalie. A woman screams behind me.

"You did this," I yell at Natalie.

She shakes her head and moves to the wall. My gun points at her chest.

"She is mine, and no one will take her from me," I say calmly, even though everything in my body is unhinged.

I pull the trigger.

Alexa is screaming, the alarm is going off now, and people are running. I hold tighter onto Alexa as Natalie slides down the wall, holding her hand against the fresh gunshot wound.

"Let's go, sweetheart," I whisper into her ear.

Cole will come, the cops will come, but it will be too late. I know what I need to do.

And I am willing to do it.

Chapter 43
Cole

Irun into the hospital; I got the call from Kolby. He was freaking out; he was fucking crying.

I never thought I would ever hear my best friend cry so hard.

I stop at the front desk. "I need you to point me toward Natalie Grey's room please," I say in a low, dark voice. My heart is racing so fast, I can hear it in my ears.

The nurse points in the direction, and I smile and nod.

I make my way down the long hallway and stop when I see my best friend come out of the room. He walks across it and hits his fist as hard as he can against the wall before he turns and slides down the wall, pulling his knees up to his chest.

I stop at his side, kneel down, and place my hand on his shoulder. He leans over, resting the side of his head against my chest, and cries. Tears escape my eyes and roll down my face. I don't know what to say or do. My heart is torn right now, between my best friend and my girl.

"Is she going to be okay?" I ask, hearing the pain in my voice. He sits up straight and looks forward into the room that is housing his girl.

A scream comes from the room, nurses rush into the room, Kolby's body stiffens.

"Physically, yes, mentally, I have no fucking clue," he confesses. He rests his head against the wall and takes a deep breath.

"I'm sorry, brother," I confess to him.

I feel like this is my fault, that all of this is my fault.

"You didn't shoot her, Cole. Don't take on guilt for something you didn't do," he says calmly. He lowers his head and turns, locking eyes with me.

I see the pain and hurt in his eyes, but no anger, not towards me anyway.

"He will pay for what he has done," I whisper.

"I know he will, but what will it cost you to do so?" He asks, continuing to look at me.

I tilt my head to the side as I search my best friend's eyes. "What do you mean?"

"Don't become the monster he wants you to become, Cole. You have fought too hard to get out of that life we once lived. Don't go back, brother," he begs me.

More tears escape my eyes and roll down my face. "I won't," I reply in a shaky voice.

"Promise me, Cole, I can't lose you. You are the only family I have," he begs and demands at the same time.

"I promise, Kolby," I confirm, knowing he needs to hear the words.

He nods and takes a deep breath. "Now go get your girl, so we all can start to put the pieces back together."

I nod and slowly stand up. I turn and look into the room. They have Natalie strapped down on the bed. My heart aches for a new reason. To see my girl's best friend in this state is something I will never forget.

I turn and start walking back down the hallway. I need to get her back. I need to make sure that this will never happen again, and now I have to figure out how to do that and also keep my promise to my best friend.

I am so fucked.

Chapter 44
Alexa

Brad pulls down the driveway. I keep looking out of the side window, holding myself tightly, as he keeps his hand on my shaking leg.

She has to be okay. Natalie can't die, she can't. I need her.

I did this. She was shot because of me. Her life is on the line because of me. Tears continue to roll down my cheek.

Brad has spoken to me about his plans for our future, saying he can go anywhere and be a lawyer for any team. He is talking as if he didn't just shoot my best friend and kidnap me. Again.

He stops the car and gets out, and I look out the window at the lake house. My heart is racing. I am sore and scared. I tuck my phone deeper into my back pocket and pull down my sweatshirt as Brad opens my door and forces me out.

"Why are you doing this?" I ask as he pulls me towards the cabin.

"Because you're mine," he states.

"I was never yours," I snap back. He stops and turns, and without saying a word, he slaps me across the face. Tears sting my eyes as he growls and opens the door, forcing me inside. As soon as we get inside, he lets go of me and pushes me onto the couch.

I can hear some voices coming from another room. The house is gorgeous. I can tell it belongs to his family from all the family pictures.

My heart stops as I slowly stand up, staring at the two men who just walked into the room. My eyes go to the man on the right. He is older, more muscular than I remember.

I shake my head. "No…No…No…"

"Hello, sweet girl," the man from my nightmares says. The man that haunts my dreams, the man that is the reason I started down the sex and drug path to begin with.

I have spent years trying to erase this man, and now, years later, he is right here in front of me.

"Darin," I whisper. He closes the distance, forcing me to sit back down on the couch. He leans down, placing his hands on either side of my head on the couch, and he rests his lips against my ear as my entire body starts to shake.

"I have been looking for you, sweet girl," he purrs, just like he did all those years ago.

My entire body has chills as he pulls back just enough to look at me, then before I can do anything, I am on my back on the couch, and he is on top of me.

"Get off, get off me," I scream.

"I always loved it when you fought me," he says with a smirk.

"What the fuck do you think you are doing?" Brad asks Darin. I turn and look at him, tears running down my face. Darin gets off the couch and grabs my arm, pulling me up. Darin walks past Brad and the other man, and starts making us go towards a room.

"No, Brad, please don't let him do this."

"Father, stop this!" Brad yells.

"It has to be done. This is how it was always supposed to be. Her parents arranged this. All of this was set in motion before you two even got together, son," the man confesses, making my heart stop.

My parents.

"No!" I scream as Darin pushes me into the bedroom, and slams the door closed behind him. He pushes me onto the bed, and I start to crawl across the bed trying to put any type of distance between us, but he has me by the ankles and pulls me back to him. Grabbing my leggings, he pulls then down and gets on top of me, shoving my face into the bed. I kick and scream, but he is too big, just like he was when I was younger.

"Just like old times, Alexa," he says with amusement.

My stomach turns into knots as he grabs my hips, putting my ass in the air. I continue to scream but the bed is stealing it from me.

I can feel his cock's head at my entrance. I try to kick, try to move down, but even from this weird position, he has all the power as he shoves himself into me. My pussy walls stretch from his large cock, him once again claiming me, shattering me.

"Oh God, you feel so good," he growls, making me feel the vomit in my throat.

I can still feel the phone. They didn't take my phone.

He will come.

He will come.

Cole will come.

I chant over and over and over again inside my head.

Darin pushes my head down one last time, as I can feel his release fill me. Tears soak the bed, his smell, and sweat is all over me, making me want to vomit.

"You are such a good fucking sweet girl for me Alexa," he purrs.

I can hear the door open and hit the wall.

"What the fuck are you doing" Darin asks. I turn my head to look, and when I do, I see Brad standing there holding a gun, pointing it right at Darin.

"She is and will always be mine, motherfucker," Brad growls as he pulls the trigger.

I slam my eyes shut, the noise from the gun making my ears ring. Darin's body falls back onto me, forcing me completely flat onto the bed. I am crying again. My sobs, smothered by the blanket, still fill the room.

"How the fuck did you get here?" Brad asks.

I can hear wrestling, banging noises, and so many footsteps.

Then someone falls to the floor.

"Alexa," I can hear Cole.

"Cole," I scream into the blanket. Darin's body gets removed from me, and before I can do anything, I am already in Cole's arms and leaving the room.

"Natalie," I cry out.

"She is in surgery," he replies as he rushes me out of the house and into the cool outside breeze.

My entire body aches as the pain comes full force, causing me to become completely unhinged.

Chapter 45
Cole

Ispeed down the highway. Alexa is in the back. She has been raped and beaten…Again. My first priority is to get her to a hospital, next is to deal with fuck nut.

We thought we got rid of him when he was sent to jail for kidnapping her the first time, but of course, his family name and money got him released on bail, and they didn't let us know. I will never ever forgive myself for not being there for her, for not being able to stop what he has done.

I look in the mirror and reach back, grabbing tightly onto her hand. She looks at me with her eye that is almost swollen shut. I can see the hand marks on her neck.

I wanted her next to me, but her groans of pain caused me even more pain. I need her to be okay; I need to know that she is going to survive this.

My car buzzes with a phone call. Mom comes across the screen. I tighten my grip on Alexa's hand as I push the button, allowing the call to go through my car.

"Mom," I say, not being able to hide the concern in my voice.

"Son, is she okay?" She asks. I can hear the tears in her tone, the sobbing just right there, but she refuses to let it out.

"I don't know," I whisper through gritted teeth.

"I can't let him use me against you, son," she confesses.

This motherfucker. I am going to kill him.

"What are you talking about?" I ask, but I already know Brad has made it clear that if I didn't walk away from Alexa that he was going to use my past, and my mother's past, against me.

"We both know what his plan is. You have worked too hard for this life for me to destroy it," she says with a sob.

"Mom, stop, you have changed. You are doing good," I say, trying to convince both of us.

Yes, I have worked hard, but now I have something worth living for, Alexa. She is my everything. Without her, none of this would matter. My life wouldn't matter.

"Right now, right now, I am doing good, but what about tomorrow, son? I can only say I will stay sober for today," she says, confessing to me.

Tears build in my eyes.

"Mom, please," I beg her.

"I have not been a good mother, but I can be now," she says with hope in her voice.

I push down on the gas, trying to get to the hospital. My emotions are going wild as I try to process what she is saying to me.

"What do you mean?"

"He can't use me if I am not in the equation," she says with confidence that sends chills down my spine.

"What the fuck does that mean, Mom?" I scream. Alexa tightens her grip on my hand, a sob leaving her.

Fuck. I look into the mirror. Her eyes are closed, and tears are running down her face.

"Let me go, son, please," she begs.

What the fuck is happening right now?

"No, fuck no."

"Son, this is for the best. You will see. Let Alexa in, okay? Don't keep her out."

"Mom"

"I love you Cole, this is for the best," she says.

My heart beats so fast I can hear it in my ears. My vision becomes blurry with the tears I can't hold back.

"I need you," I whisper.

"She needs you more," she whispers.

Bang.

"Mom," I scream.

Cries fill my car as I turn into the hospital. I put the car in park, open the door, get out, and open the back, gently grabbing Alexa. She grabs the back of my neck as I bring her against me. She sobs into my chest, both of us unable to hold back the tears.

We are both crying, for two reasons, both of us feeling the impact of what just happened, of what has happened.

I thought I could control the outcome; I thought I could outsmart him, but in the end, he has always been two fucking steps ahead of me.

I run into the ER, the same one that she used to work at. The staff stops as I drop to my knees in the middle of the ER. She shoves her face into the side of my neck, making my heart ache.

"Please help her," I cry out, my entire body shaking.

The staff rush to us, taking her from my arms. I release my grip on her, allowing them to take her away from me. I quickly stand and grab her hand. As they set her on the bed, they begin to roll her toward a room.

"Cole," Kolby screams my name, getting my attention. I turn my head to the right and he runs to my side. He looks down at Alexa, then at me, and all I can do is shake my head as the nurse stops me by placing her hand on my chest, shaking her head, forcing me to let go of Alexa's hand.

"We have her, I promise," she whispers as she turns and closes the curtain.

I can hear Alexa's sobs as my knees give out, and I fall to the ground. Kolby wraps his arms around me from behind. He falls down with me as I lean forward, gripping tightly to his arms as I let out a scream.

The entire ER goes silent as the tears escape me, the pain consuming me, the rage, the darkness taking over me.

"I got you, Cole, I got you," Kolby whispers as I force us both to rock back and forth.

Everything is racing inside my head, every single thing that has happened in the last several months.

I failed them both.

Tears continue to run down my face as Brad's face enters my mind, his voice in my ear, his words haunting me.

I lift my head and slowly stand up, forcing Kolby to let me go. I turn and look at my best friend.

"Please watch over her for me," I ask, pleading with him.

He slowly nods.

"What are you going to do, Cole?" He asks in a concerned voice.

I take a deep breath, locking eyes with my best friend. "I will shatter him like fucking ice."

He nods and places his hand on Natalie's lower back, leading her into the space where they are holding Alexa, my beautiful baby girl.

I turn and start to walk towards the exit sign.

He will pay for what he has done, I will make sure of it.

The last place I saw Brad was when I knocked him out at the lake house. I don't know if he will still be there, but it is a good place to start.

I speed down the gravel road and stop in front of the house of horrors. Brad killed the man that was raping my girl. Now I need to finish off Brad. This has to end. It can't keep going like this, or none of us will survive in the end.

My phone buzzes as I turn off the car. I look down at my phone, and my heart stops when I see Kolby's message.

Alexa is gone

What do you mean gone?

Natalie and I stepped out for a moment to get coffee, and when we came back, she was gone. I'm sorry, brother.

Fuck, fuck, fuck.

I slam my hands against the steering wheel and take a big, deep breath.

This ends today.

Chapter 46
Brad

The alarm goes off as I continue to sit on the bed, looking down at Darin's dead body. Once again, she was taken from me. This is nothing but a fucking shit show. My father is in the wind, and I do not know what to do.

I knew Cole would come for me. He wouldn't love her if he didn't.

This will end today one way or another, and if I can't have it my way, neither one of us will have her.

I hear footsteps getting closer as I stand and rest the pistol against my head. "It took you long enough, Cole," I say calmly as I look up at him.

His hands are in fists at his sides, and his shirt is dirty and has blood on it from when he took Alexa away from me, leaving me in a daze on the floor.

"Who was he?" He asks.

I tilt my head to the side. "She never told you?"

He shakes his head.

"My father said he is the first man that ever had your baby girl, my sweetheart," I say, watching him closely.

He growls at the dead body, then takes a step closer to me. I raise the gun at him, a smirk crossing my face.

"I wanted so badly to make her mine, but now I just want to make sure that if I can't have her, you can't either," I confess softly.

"You never had her, Brad. You are weak. Look at you, needing a gun, because you can't beat me in a fair fight," he mocks, but it won't work.

"I had some lovely talks with your mother. She broke pretty easily. I wonder if it will be as easy to break you with my words as it was for me to break her?" I ask.

"Leave her out of this!" He screams.

"Too late. I told her I would use her against you, destroy your name, your hockey career. She really cares about you, just got off the phone with her, actually, not that long ago," I taunt.

His body is shaking. My words are affecting him, just like I knew they would. "You aren't as strong as you may think, Cole Jackson," I continue to prod.

"Neither are you. What type of man needs to kidnap and rape a woman to make her his?" He growls back.

Fuck, nice move.

"I did what I had to do. She will never forget me," I say with a smile.

"She will," he says with confidence that makes my blood boil.

"She won't, because if I die, you are dying with me," I say, taking a small step forward, but he doesn't move. There is still too much distance for us to touch each other, but a bullet will work just fine.

Chapter 47
Alexa

Brad has lied to me since the beginning, telling me he has my best interest at heart, that all the changes would help me see myself in a better light, that it would help with my self-esteem and self-worth.

But it was all a lie.

He just wanted someone that he could mold into what he wanted, someone that he could make submit to him, that made him look good. I never understood why he chose me, but now I get it.

My parents, they hate me, they still hate me, and they wanted to give me to Darin. That much I know from what Brad's father confessed at the lake house.

I don't know how they knew we would meet to set this all up, but one thing I know about my parents is that they will do whatever they have to do to get what they want, and they don't care who they hurt in the process.

They have told me I was destroying our name in the publishing world and that I needed to be a good daughter and just do as I am told. They hated that I didn't mold into what they wanted. They thought I would mold into what Brad wanted, and they almost got what they wanted, but I can promise you my parents never saw Cole coming.

Because of Cole, I am free, and I will not let him go to prison or die because of me, because of my family.

I will protect him, like he has protected me, even if it means that I have to give my life for his.

I slowly make my way into the bedroom where the man of my nightmares lay dead on the floor. Stopping a few inches inside the door, I raise the gun in a shaking hand as I look at Brad, who has a gun pointed at Cole. Cole is between us, but off to the side. He reaches out his hand to me; I grab it, and he pulls me into him. I melt against his strong body as tears sting my eyes. I watch Brad and he is starting to pace while keeping his gun trained on Cole.

"You won't shoot me, Alexa. You don't have it in you," Brad taunts.

"You changed me. Darin has changed me. I won't let you take the one thing that matters to me, Brad," I confess, allowing him to see my love for Cole.

"You are choosing him over me? After I killed Darin for you," he says in an insulted voice.

"After he raped me! And you didn't do it for me, you did it for you, because you think you have some claim to me," I snap, feeling the rage consuming me.

"I do," he says, trying to convince me of his lies, but it won't fucking work, not anymore.

"No, you don't," I say through gritted teeth as I steady my hand.

"You will never forget me, sweetheart," he says with confidence, confidence that will be shattered when I prove him wrong.

"You're wrong. He has already replaced you," I whisper.

"Noooo," Brad screams as he steps forward.

My finger pulls the trigger.

Bang…Bang…Bang.

Three times, three times it hits him in the chest.

His body stills, his eyes are on me as he drops his gun and falls to his knees as he grips his chest. "You bitch," he whispers as he falls forward onto his face.

I drop the gun, my knees give out, and Cole wraps his arms around me as I fall to the ground, taking him with me.

I lean forward, resting my forehead on the floor. I let out a painful scream.

It had to be done; he was going to take Cole from me. And I couldn't let that happen.

"I got you, baby girl, I got you," he whispers as he rests his face against mine.

His warmth.

His scent.

His love consumes me, taking me away from the fact that I am now a murderer.

Chapter 48
Cole

Idon't feel the rain as it falls down on me. I hold tightly onto the roses in my hand and kneel in front of the grave. I place the roses on top of the fresh dirt that fills the hole holding my mother.

She was a good mother. She didn't always make the best choices, and she battled her demons of addiction her entire life, but when it came down to it, she was always there for me, and in the end, she made sure she saved me instead of herself.

"Thank you for giving your life for me mom, I promise I will make you proud," I promise as I set my right hand on the dirt, and lower my head, tears fall from my eyes, as her last words flood my head.

The rain falls harder, soaking my shirt as I slowly stand and place my hands in my front pockets. I can hear the footsteps behind me. Stopping beside me, I take in a deep breath as Kolby rests his hand on my shoulder, giving it a squeeze.

"She did the one thing she could, Cole. She gave her life for you because she loved you very much," he says calmly and with confidence.

"I know she did." I smile and nod.

"We will make sure she didn't die for nothing," he confesses softly.

Kolby pulls out his phone and answers it. "Hey baby," he says calmly.

I turn and look at my best friend as he looks down at the grave, and then up at the sky, taking a deep breath.

"We are on our way," he says to her, then hangs up.

"Alexa?" I ask, but I already know.

"We need to go brother, your girl needs you, and mine needs me," he says, squeezing my shoulder one last time.

I nod and kneel back down, placing my hand once again on the dirt.

"I love you, mom," I sob.

I stand up again and turn, watching my best friend head towards his truck.

I will make her proud. I will be the man I know I can and need to be to put back together the pieces.

This is not the end for us, but just the beginning. The road of healing will be rough as fuck, but Alexa has me, and I am never leaving her.

Like I said at the beginning, I will always be what she needs.

Chapter 49
Cole

Ibang on the bathroom door. She has been in there for hours with the water running. She has refused to answer the door several times, and I am trying to be understanding, I am trying to give her the space she needs, but I can't do it anymore, she doesn't need this much space, what she needs is me, and I am right here, right fucking here if only she will let me in.

"Baby girl, please open the door," I beg her, as I continue to bang on the door.

"Go away," she demands. I can hear the pain in her voice, her words sting, sting so fucking much.

"No, open this damn door. I am right here, you hear me?" I say against the door.

"Just leave Cole, go, you are free," she says with darkness in her tone.

The fuck?

"What? I don't want to be free, I want you, I want you Alexa," I confess to her, hoping she fucking can hear me.

My words are true.

"I am not worth all of this," she screams.

"Open this damn door or I will break it down," I snap.

The door swings open, and standing in front of me is Alexa. She is in a crop top and shorts. Her body sways as she takes another big gulp from the bottle.

I have never seen her drunk; in fact, I have never seen her drink at all.

"What are you doing?" I ask as I enter the bathroom. She stands still and looks me over, then takes another big gulp.

"Drowning out my darkness," she confesses.

"Is it working?"

She shakes her head. "Not yet, but it will. Just give me time," she says, as she takes another gulp.

I reach out my hand and she looks at it as she takes another drink. I take a small step forward.

"Give it to me," I demand.

"Fuck you," she says as she turns and takes another big gulp. I come up behind her, wrapping my arms around her as I grab the bottle.

"Let go," she screams.

"Alexa, let the bottle go."

"Fuck you, Cole," she screams as she leans forward, trying to get it away from me. I let go, and she stands up and looks at me in the mirror.

"You see what I am, Cole? Leave," she screams.

"I am not going anywhere," I whisper, watching her closely.

Her breathing is unsteady and uneven as she screams and throws the bottle at the mirror. Both of them shatter. She turns around and looks at me, tears rolling down her beautiful face.

She walks into me. "You don't want this."

"Don't tell me what I want or don't want," I say through gritted teeth, her eyes rapidly search mine.

I grab her throat and pull her completely into me. "I want you, and I will be whatever you need me to be. Tell me, what do you need, and I will give it to you," I beg her.

"Cole," she sobs.

"Baby girl," I plead with her.

"It hurts," she cries.

"Where?" I ask.

"Here," she points at her chest, making my heart shatter.

I wrap my arms tightly around her. She melts into me, shoving her face into my chest.

"Let it out. I am here. I am not going anywhere, I promise." I kiss the top of her head as she cries into my chest, letting the pain out on my shirt.

I would die for this girl, and I refuse to let her drown in her darkness alone. I will drown with her.

Always.

Chapter 50
Cole

Irest my hands on the counter and lower my head, taking a deep breath. It is 2 A.M. and I can't sleep because I don't know what Alexa would do if I did. I can't trust her alone with herself right now.

Which is why I have a fucking baby monitor in our room facing her, and the last time I checked, she was asleep.

I take in a deep, shaky breath. "She will heal, she will get through this, Cole," Natalie whispers as she stops beside me, resting her hand on top of mine.

"I don't know what to do, Nat. I am scared I will lose her."

"You won't. She loves you, Cole."

"I know, but what if the darkness around her is stronger than I am?"

I look over at Nat. She shakes her head. "It isn't. Do you know who Darin was to her, Cole?"

"No," I say, shaking my head. I stand up straight and lean against the counter, crossing my arms over my chest. Nat takes in a deep breath.

"Natalie's parents had a family friend named Darin. He has been in her life since she was young. They called him uncle, but he wasn't blood. Her family is one of the biggest names in the publishing world, and he has some black market favors that have helped them get where they are," she says calmly, looking into my eyes.

"Okay, go on," I beg her softly.

She takes another deep breath and leans against the counter.

"When she was about fifteen years old, he started coming around more and more, especially when her parents were out making business deals, focusing on their dreams instead of their daughter. He was interested in Alexa," she confesses, her voice cracking a little bit.

Interested?

"Interested how?" I ask, already knowing the answer, but I need to hear it.

"He wanted her, and her parents offered her to him, to keep her in line. He started having his way with her. She told her parents, and her mother told her it wasn't true, even though she knew very well it was, since she was the one who offered her daughter to him in the first place."

"Why the fuck would they do that?"

"He had connections and money, and they wanted their publishing company."

"Seriously?"

She nods as tears start to fall down her face. "After years of abuse and rape by his hands, Alexa started to search for an escape. She found it in booze, drugs, and men," she says in a low, shaky voice.

My heart stops as her words sink in.

"So that is why she was guarded?"

She nods, "Yes, and when she could, she escaped, and we moved in together. We both come from darkness. I was there for hers, and she was there for mine. We both ran from our pasts," Natalie says with more tears.

"I would never hurt her."

"I know that, and she knows that, but you have to understand the only person who has never left her is me; you have to show her that you mean what you say."

"How?"

"By doing exactly what you are doing, refuse to leave, push her boundaries, hold her, love her."

"I will," I nod, doing my best to reassure her.

"I know you will, just know though, if you ever hurt her, I will kill you," she says with a smile.

A chuckle leaves me. "I believe you."

She smiles and nods and pushes off the counter, making her way to the doorway.

"You are good for him, you know."

"No, he is the one who is good for me," she confesses as she leaves the kitchen.

I push off the counter and make my way back down the hallway to my bedroom. I open and close the door, crawling back into bed with my everything, my ice.

I hold her close and allow her scent and warmth to cover me.

I will protect her, even if I have to protect her from herself.

Chapter 51
Cole

"If I can't have her, no one will," Brad says with confidence.

My heart races as I see the gun, as I see the love of my life. At this moment I don't know what to do, I don't know how to fix this.

Everything has led to this moment. I should have done more. I should have stopped him. It never should have ever gotten to this point.

Alexa is holding the gun steady, and so is Brad.

I want to get between them; I want to protect her, but I don't know how. I am frozen, fucking terrified that after all this time, I am going to lose her; I need her, and she needs me.

It can't end this like, it can't fucking end like this.

"Alexa," I scream out as I sit up in bed. Sweat and tears cover me. I turn and look over at my ice. She is sitting up with a knife in her hand.

Blood is all over the blanket, sheets, and her.

"What the fuck?" I scream as I scramble to her, taking the knife from her. She rests her back against the bedframe, and I grab her arm and a sheet.

"Baby girl," I cry.

"It is better this way. You need to be free. I am letting you be free," she mumbles. I can tell she has been bleeding for far too long.

"Baby, please, hang on, I can't lose you, Kolby, Natalie," I scream at the top of my lungs.

I can hear the footsteps, but everything is fading except for her.

I sit back in the chair, holding the love of my life's hand. I feel like I should do more, but there is nothing for me to do but sit here and be here for her the best I can.

I look down at her bandaged arm. They stopped the bleeding and put her on an IV drip. They had to strap her down on the bed. She was losing control of her emotions. Hearing her scream, begging them to let her die, ripped me the fuck apart.

Kolby found a suicide note in my room, her telling me I am better off without her. She doesn't realize that I can't live without her; I refuse to live without her.

"Cole," she groans, turning her head towards me.

"I got you, baby girl. I am right here," I say, leaning forward, rubbing her forehead with my thumb.

"I'm sorry."

"You have nothing to be sorry for, baby," I tell her, needing her to hear me.

"Yes, I do."

I hold back my tears as I rest my forehead against hers. "Promise me you will never leave me, Alexa. I can't live in a world where you don't exist," I beg her and demand.

"I promise," she says softly, making my heart beat faster.

"We do this together," I plead with her.

"Together," she says with a smile. I slowly crawl onto the bed, taking her into my arms as I rest against the back of the bed. She melts into me and starts to nod out again.

There is nothing I wouldn't do for this girl, because without her, I am nothing.

The Fame.

The money.

The position.

All of it means nothing if she isn't in this life with me.

Chapter 52
Cole

Iopen the house door and make my way into the kitchen, grabbing a water from the fridge. Training was brutal, but it went great, actually. We feel more and more like family every day, and so far, no one has been able to come close to our teamwork. It is why no one has beaten us yet.

The next game is next weekend against Denver, and they have a strong defense, but I am confident we will be able to show them just how hard we are to beat.

I take a few gulps of water and look down at the floor in the hallway. It is covered in pink rose petals. I set down the water and make my way down the hallway into my bedroom and stop when I see the candles, and a few things on the bed. I slowly enter.

"Alexa," I whisper as I stop in front of the bed. I look down and see a test, a letter, a pink rose, and a baby outfit. My heart stops as I grab the note.

Cole,

You saved me, just like I know I saved you. Baby, I am so proud of you. I love you so much. Thank you for never giving up on me. You are going to be an amazing father.

Tears fill my eyes as my knees give out, and I fall down at the side of the bed, grabbing the positive test.

I turn when I hear the bathroom door open, and standing in a pink dress, her dark brown hair in a messy bun is my ice.

I can tell she was crying, but her eyes tell me they were happy tears. They *are* happy tears. Tears escape my eyes and roll down my face as she makes her way over to me, kneeling down beside me.

"Is this real?" I ask.

She smiles and nods.

"I'm going to be a dad?"

"You are going to be a dad," she confirms.

I drop the test and turn, grabbing her face; I smash my lips against hers. She opens up for me, allowing my tongue to enter. A moan escapes her as I move in such a way that she lays down on her back I get between her legs. She grabs my sweats and pulls them down, and I release her face, keeping our lips connected as she pulls them down my body. I grab my already hard cock and place the tip at her entrance.

I pull back just enough to look at her.

"I love you, baby girl. "

"I love you too," she says softly as I push myself inside her. Her pussy wraps tightly around my cock as I place one hand on her throat and the other next to her head. She rests her hands against my chest and wraps her legs around my waist as I start to move in and out of her.

Both of us getting lost in the moment.

This beautiful moment.

I am going to be a father; she is going to be a mother.

All of the pieces are finally coming back together again.

Chapter 53
Cole
1 Year Later

Once again, it all comes down to this moment, the moment that will define the whole season. If we win this, we will win the Gold Cup again. This is what we have been working our asses off for, and it all comes down to this last play.

My heart is racing as I look down at the ice, the one thing that used to keep me stable, the only thing I had to hang onto, but now I have the ice and so much more. I turn and look over at the stands; I see Natalie, and next to her is my beautiful wife, and our six-month-old son Carsen.

We didn't know that she was pregnant with my child at first; it was a blessing, a surprise that saved us. Saved my wife. She was in a dark place after killing Brad, and I was trying to keep her from drowning. I felt like I was losing her.

Then we found out she was pregnant, and everything changed for both of us.

The buzzer goes off, and everyone goes crazy, the players and the fans as I move from side to side with the puck. I hit it hard to the left, to Wright, and he takes off down the ice. I ram hard into one of the players, and try to stay side by side with him.

"Wright," I scream his name. He hits the puck hard my way. I move it side to side as I come within a few feet of the goalie.

I take a deep breath and hit it with everything I have. Letting out a battle scream, I slide to the left, watching the puck go across the ice and right between his legs as the buzzer goes off.

The fans go crazy, my team all making their way towards me as my knees give out and I fall to the ice.

"Baby," Alexa whispers. I look up and see my wife kneeling down with our son in her arms. Her eyes are filled with tears.

"Baby girl," I whisper with a sob, all my emotions coming together as one in this moment.

"I am so proud of you," she says with a smile.

"I love you," I sob out.

"I love you, too," she says with a smile.

This woman is my everything. None of this would be possible without her or my son.

They both have become my ice.

Once we were shattered, and now we have put each other back together again.

Just like perfectly groomed ice before a game.

Chapter 54
Melting Ice
Prologue

I take a deep breath as I sign across the line, the line that will change everything. It took me a long time to get to this moment, the moment of signing this line, and all of this to be over.

Signing the papers has always been on my mind; I became obsessed.

There comes a time in everyone's life when they have to do what is best for them and not what is best for everyone else.

I couldn't take the distance anymore and felt a lack of desire, need, and passion.

It took me months to accept that it was over between us, but that doesn't make it less painful.

When you give your life and your heart to someone and, in the end, it is wasted. It is a kind of pain that can't put into words.

He has always been different in our relationship, something I accepted a long time ago, but I never thought we would turn into this.

Two people share the house, even the same last name, but everything else is separate.

How can someone live without the other? Who does their laundry and their grocery shopping, and comes together at night for a few hours, but still the words between us were limited?

But here we are, both of us signing the on the dotted line admitting we are done, and it is time to go our separate ways.

This is not a story of how easy it is to start over or how easy it is to walk away from someone you will always love, but are no longer in love with.

This is a story of a woman who chose herself instead of him.

This is a story of a woman who actually chose to be happy instead of making him happy.

This is a story of starting over and how taboo love can smack you right in the face and take you for a wild ride when you least expect it.

This is my story, how the darkness was drowning me, and the light I never thought would find me in the form of a man I never saw coming.

Melting ice will have a whole new meaning; I can promise you that.

About Author

Sasha R.C. is quickly becoming recognized as The Queen of Dark Romance. She overcame her addiction to alcohol and drugs and now lives a life of recovery, all thanks to her higher power and her strong support system of family and friends. She now reaches out to help others overcome that same addiction as an alcohol and drug counselor.

Sasha loves getting lost in a good Dark Romance book. Her favorites include Den of Vipers, Church, The Ritual, The Sinner, The Sacrifice, The Joker, The Psycho, The Reaper, Haunting Adeline, and Hunting Adeline.

Sasha currently resides in Washington.

Sasha is currently working on a lot of different dark standalone romances, so stay tuned.

Thank you for taking the time to read Shattered Ice.

Please consider leaving a review on Amazon.

Come follow me on social media: sasharcauthor

TikTok

Instagram

Twitter

Facebook

www.authorsashachristophersen.org

Other Books by Sasha R.C.

The Born Trilogy – A Dark Why Choose Vampire Romance

Ripped	Souls	Book	1
Ripped	Hearts	Book	2
Ripped Destiny Book 3			

The Fated Trilogy- A Dark Why Choose Werewolf MC Romance

Blood   Beast   MC   Book   1

Blood   Beast   MC   Book   2

Blood Beast MC Book 3

The Crown Trilogy- A Dark Why Choose Witch Romance

Covenant   of   the   Crown   Book   1

Covenant   of   the   Crown   Book   2

Covenant of the Crown Book 3

The Shadow Trilogy- A Dark Why Choose FAE Romance

Queen   of   the   Shadows   Book   1

Queen   of   the   Shadows   Book   2

Queen   of   the   Shadows   Book   3

Standalone in Same Universe – The Forgotten Dragon – A Dark Why Choose Dragon Romance

The Secret Praise Series – A Dark Why Choose Bully College Romance

Standalone:

Awakened Craving – A Dark Taboo Forbidden Romance

CrissCrossed – A Dark Why Choose High School Bully   Romance

Kiss of Sin – A Dark Love Triangle Romance

Unworthy of Your Love – A Dark Why Choose Romance

Broken Like Me – A Dark Why Choose College Romance

Fatal Vows – A Dark Why Choose DV Romance

Him   and   I   –   A   Dark   Romance

Fatal Attraction – A Dark Why Choose Mafia Romance

Our Beautiful Creature – A Dark Why Choose Retelling   Romance

Dark   Souls   –   A   Dark   MC   Romance

Silent   Tears   –   A   Dark   Mafia   Romance

Blood Tears – A Dark Revenge Romance

beautiful Beasts – A Dark Beauty and the Beast Retelling Romance

Sinful Touch – A Dark Taboo Romance

Chapter 55
Other Books by Sasha R.C.